Dear Reader,

Great news—in February 2013 Harlequin Presents Extra is merging with Presents so you will now be able to find more of your favorite authors in one place as Presents increases from six books a month to eight.

There will be more of the themes you love such as secret babies, marriages of convenience, scandalous affairs, all with exciting international settings and delicious alpha heroes. You can also look forward to linked books by some of your most-loved authors and a new exciting eight-book continuity starting in May.

So remember, starting in February there will be eight new Presents books available each month!

Happy reading!

The Presents Editors

P.S. Also available this month:

#3107 A RING TO SECURE HIS HEIR
Lynne Graham

#3108 THE RUTHLESS CALEB WILDE
The Wilde Brothers
Sandra Marton

#3109 BEHOLDEN TO THE THRONE
Empire of the Sands
Carol Marinelli

#3110 THE INCORRIGIBLE PLAYBOY
The Legendary Finn Brothers
Emma Darcy

#3111 BENEATH THE VEIL OF PARADISE
The Bryants: Powerful & Proud
Kate Hewitt

#3112 AT HIS MAJESTY'S REQUEST
The Call of Duty
Maisey Yates

"Alex, you don't want me as a wife and you don't want to be a father, either. I can *feel* that reluctance in you," Rosie muttered with emphasis, her wide green eyes troubled but open.

"You don't need to pretend otherwise with me. I'm just as shocked as you are about the baby, but we don't have to get married to do the right thing—for a start I couldn't fit into your world. Your friends would laugh at me. I'd embarrass you. I'm a cleaner, for goodness' sake!"

"Nobody would laugh at you while I was around," Alexius ground out forcefully, sending a quiver of awareness running down her spine. "I would make a real effort to be a good husband and father—"

"But you don't love me…and to have you *trying* all the time would be very hard on my self-esteem," Rosie protested.

Alexius threw her a derisive look that stung. "Love is lust, nothing more and I can assure you that in that department I'm unlikely to disappoint you."

Lynne Graham

A RING TO SECURE HIS HEIR

HARLEQUIN®

entertain, enrich, inspire™

Recycling programs
for this product may
not exist in your area.

ISBN-13: 978-0-373-13113-6

A RING TO SECURE HIS HEIR

First North American Publication 2013

www.Harlequin.com

Printed in U.S.A.

All about the author…
Lynne Graham

Of Irish/Scottish parentage, **LYNNE GRAHAM** has lived in
Northern Ireland all her life. She has one brother. She grew up in
a seaside village and now lives in a country house surrounded by a
woodland garden, which is wonderfully private.

Lynne met her husband when she was fourteen; they married after
she completed a degree at Edinburgh University. Lynne wrote
her first book at fifteen—it was rejected everywhere. She started
writing again when she was home with her first child. It took several
attempts before she was published, and she has never forgotten the
delight of seeing that book for sale at the local newsagents.

Lynne always wanted a large family, and she now has five children.
Her eldest, her only natural child, is in her twenties and is a
university graduate. Her other children, who are every bit as
dear to her heart, are adopted: two from Sri Lanka and two from
Guatemala. In Lynne's home, there is a rich and diverse cultural
mix, which adds a whole extra dimension of interest and discovery
to family life.

The family has two pets. Thomas, a very large and affectionate
black cat, bosses the dog and hunts rabbits. The dog is Daisy, an
adorable but not very bright West Highland white terrier, who loves
being chased by the cat. At night, the dog and cat sleep together in
front of the kitchen stove.

Lynne loves gardening and cooking, collects everything from old
toys to rock specimens and is crazy about every aspect of Christmas.

Other titles by Lynne Graham available in ebook:

Harlequin Presents®

CHAPTER ONE

'I NEED a favour,' Socrates Seferis had said and his god-son, Alexius Stavroulakis, had dropped everything to fly thousands of miles to come to his aid. Socrates had been strangely mysterious about the nature of the favour, declaring that it was a highly confidential matter that he couldn't discuss on the phone.

Alexius, six feet one in bare feet and built like a professional athlete, was a very newsworthy billionaire of only thirty-one years of age with a fleet of bodyguards, limousines, properties and private jets at his disposal. Famed for his tough tactics in business and a naturally aggressive nature, Alexius never danced to anyone else's tune, but Socrates Seferis, although he was almost seventy-five years old, was a special case. For many years he had been the only visitor Alexius had had while at boarding school in the UK.

A self-made businessman, Socrates was a hardworking multimillionaire with a string of tourist hotels round the world. Alexius's godfather, however, had not been so fortunate in his private life. The wife Socrates adored had died during the birth of their third child and the old man's kids had grown into adult horrors, who were spoiled, lazy and extravagant and who had on many occasions shamed their kind-hearted, honourable father beyond bearing. Alexius considered Socrates an excellent example of why no sensible man should have children. Children were often disloyal, distressing and difficult and he had no idea why some of his friends were so keen to have the little blighters cluttering up lives that, childfree, could have remained blessedly smooth and civilised. It was not a mistake that Alexius planned to make.

Socrates greeted Alexius from his armchair on the terrace of his luxurious home on the outskirts of Athens. Refreshments arrived before the younger man even got seated.

'So,' Alexius prompted, his lean, darkly handsome features serious, the silvery-grey eyes that made women melt shrewd and cool as always. 'What's wrong?'

'You never did learn patience, did you?' the old man quipped, his bright dark eyes sparkling with humour in his weather-beaten face. 'Have a drink, read the file first…'

Impatience bubbling through his big powerful frame, Alexius scooped up the slim file on the table and opened it, ignoring the drink. The head and shoulders photo of a pale, nondescript girl who looked barely out of her teens was uppermost. 'Who is she?'

'Read,' Socrates reminded his godson doggedly.

His breath escaping in a slow hiss of exasperation, Alexius flipped through the thin file. The name Rosie Gray meant nothing to him and the more he read the less he understood the relevance of the information.

'She calls herself Rosie,' Socrates mused abstractedly. 'My late wife was English too. She was christened Rose as well.'

Alexius was baffled by what he had gleaned from the file. Rosie Gray was an English girl who had grown up in care in London and worked as a humble cleaner, living, on the face of it, a very ordinary life. He could see no possible reason for his godfather's interest in her.

'She's my granddaughter,' Socrates supplied as though Alexius had spoken.

Alexius shot him an incredulous look. 'Since when? Is this woman trying to con you or something?'

'You're *definitely* the right man for the job,' Socrates informed his godson with satisfaction. 'No, she's not trying to con me, Alexius. As far as I'm aware, she doesn't even know I exist. I'm curious about her…that's why I asked you here to talk to me.'

Alexius's eyes skimmed back to the photo: a plain Jane if ever he saw one, with pale hair, big empty eyes and no visible personality. 'Why do you think she's your granddaughter?'

'I know it for a fact. I've known she existed for more than fifteen years and she was DNA tested then,' Socrates admitted grudgingly. 'She's Troy's child, conceived while he was working for me in London—not that he did much work while he was over there,' he added with a humourless laugh. 'He didn't marry the girl's mother either. In fact, he had already abandoned them before he died. The woman contacted me looking for financial support and I made a substantial settlement on her and the little girl, but for whatever reasons the girl herself saw none of that money and the mother left her to grow up in foster homes.'

'Unfortunate,' Alexius remarked.

'Worse than unfortunate. The girl has grown up with every possible disadvantage and I feel very guilty about that,' the older man admitted heavily. 'She *is* family and she could be my heir—'

Alexius was alarmed by that staggering declaration. 'Your *heir*? A girl you've never even met? What about the family you already have?'

'My daughter has no children and a spending habit that none of her three rich husbands have been able to afford,' Socrates responded flatly. 'My surviving son is a drug addict, as you know, and he has been in rehab repeatedly without success—'

'But you do have a couple of grandsons.'

'As spendthrift and unreliable as their parents. My grandsons are, as we speak, under suspicion of having committed fraud in one of my hotels. I don't intend to leave any of them out of my will,' Socrates volunteered heavily, 'but if this granddaughter is a suitable person I will leave her the bulk of my money.'

'What do you mean by a "suitable person"?' Alexius asked with a frown.

'If she's a decent girl with her heart in the right place, she'll be welcome to make her home here with me. You're a man of honour and restraint and I trust you to judge her character for me—'

'*Me*? What have I got to do with this business? Why can't you fly over there and meet the girl for yourself?' Alexius demanded, his black brows drawing together in confusion.

'I have decided against doing that. Anyone can put up a convincing front for a couple of days. She'd soon see that it would be in her own best interests to impress me.' The old man sighed heavily, a lifetime of cynicism and too many disappointments etched in his troubled face. 'I've too much at stake to trust my own judgement—

I desperately want her to be different from the rest of my family. My children have lied to me and betrayed me over money and other matters too many times to count, Alexius. I don't want to get my hopes up about this girl and run the risk of being fooled again. Nor do I need another scrounger hanging on to my coat-tails.'

'I'm afraid I still don't understand quite what you expect me to do about the situation,' Alexius admitted levelly.

'I want you to check Rosie out for me before I take the chance of getting involved with her.'

'Check her out?' Alexius leapt on the phrase. 'You want me to have her investigated again?'

'No, I want you to meet her, get to know her, size her up for me,' Socrates confided with a hopeful look in his steady gaze. 'This means a lot to me, Alex.'

'You can't be serious? You're asking me to get to know…a *cleaner*?' Alexius prompted in flaring disbelief.

The old man looked grave. 'I have never thought of you as a snob.'

Alexius stiffened and wondered how he could possibly be anything else with his background. After all, generations of very wealthy blue-blooded Greeks filled out his now much diminished family tree. 'What could we possibly have in common? And how could I set up such a meeting without her guessing that something strange lay behind my interest?'

'Hire the cleaning firm she works for… I'm sure if you think about it, you'll come up with other ideas,' Socrates Seferis asserted confidently. 'I know it's a big favour and that you're very busy but I don't have anyone else I could ask or trust. Do I approach my son—

her uncle—or one of her untrustworthy cousins to take care of this for me?'

'No, that would not be fair. They would view another family member coming out of the woodwork as competition.'

'Exactly.' Socrates looked relieved by the younger man's quick understanding. 'I will be deeply in your debt if you take care of this matter for me. If Rose's namesake turns out to be greedy or dishonest you need never tell me the unsavoury details. I only need to know if she's a worthwhile risk.'

'I'll consider it,' Alexius pronounced grudgingly.

'Don't take too long—I'm not getting any younger,' Socrates warned him.

'Is there something I should know about?' Alexius prompted tautly, worried that Socrates had health concerns that he was keeping secret. Alexius was touched by the faith the older man had in his judgement but he still didn't want the job, which sixth sense warned him would be a solid gold poisoned chalice. 'You have other friends—'

'None as shrewd or experienced as you are with women,' Socrates countered gravely. 'You will know her for what she is. I'm convinced she won't succeed in pulling the wool over your eyes.'

Alexius finally lifted his drink and sighed, 'I'll think this over. Are you well?'

The old man gave him a stubborn appraisal. 'There is nothing that you need worry about.'

Nonetheless, Alexius was filled with concern, but the closed look of obstinacy on Socrates's face kept him from demanding answers to that laden assurance. He was already disconcerted by Socrates's abnormally frank speech. His godfather had buried his pride and virtually bared his soul when he openly admitted for the first time what a disappointment his three adult children had proved to be. Alexius perfectly understood that the old man did not want to add another idle freeloader to his family circle, but he could not approve of his devious approach to the problem.

'Suppose this girl is the good granddaughter that you want?' Alexius prompted uneasily. 'How will she feel when she finds out about your relationship and realises that I'm your godson? She'll know then that she was set up—'

'And she'll understand *why* if she ever meets the rest of my family,' Socrates fielded without anxiety. 'It's not a perfect plan, Alexius, but it's the only way I can face the possibility of letting her into my life.'

Having dined with his godfather, Alexius flew straight back to London in an unusually troubled state of mind. He lived for the challenge of business, the action of staying one step ahead of his closest competitors and the thrill of ensuring that his enemies fell by the wayside. What the hell did he know about working out whether or not his godfather's long-lost granddaughter was a fit person to become the old man's heir? It was a huge responsibility and an unwelcome challenge when Alexius did not consider himself to be 'a people person'.

Indeed, his own private life was as regimented as his public life. He didn't like ties and he gave his trust to very few. He had no family of his own to consider and believed that lack had simply made him tougher. His relationships were never complicated and, with women, were generally so basic that sometimes they filled even him with distaste. He had always avoided the ones who wanted commitment, and the other ones, the habitually shallow beauties who shared his bed, often put a price on their bodies that would have shamed a hooker. But he was a not a hypocrite even if he was aware that on one level he did pay for their services with the heady allure of the publicity being seen in his company offered and with the designer clothes, diamonds and the luxurious lifestyle he supplied. All such women had a natural talent for feathering their own nests and their greed was no worse, to his own mind, than his body's natural need for sexual release.

'So what's so special about this job?' Zoe demanded impatiently. 'Why do we have to move here?'

Rosie suppressed a sigh as the two young women wheeled the cleaning trolley through the almost silent foyer into the lift, having shown their identification to the security staff on the doors. 'STA Industries is part of a much bigger concern and this may only be a small contract but this *is* their headquarters. Vanessa is convinced that if we provide an efficient service here it could lead to more work and she chose us because she says we're her best workers.'

The attractive brunette by Rosie's side grimaced, unimpressed by the compliment. 'We may be her best workers but she doesn't pay us on that basis and it'll cost me more to travel here.'

Rosie was no more enamoured of the change in her routine, but in the current economic climate she was relieved to still have regular employment, not to mention the invaluable accommodation that went with the job. After all, only a week ago Rosie had found herself unex-

pectedly and scarily homeless and only Vanessa's offer
of a room had saved Rosie and her pet dog, Baskerville,
from ending up on the street with their possessions. It
would be quite some time before she stopped being
grateful for her reasonably priced bedsit in a building
rented by her employer and shared with other staff.

Vanessa Jansen's office-cleaning business was small
and she only got contracts by severely undercutting her
competitors, which meant that the profits were minimal
and the contents of Rosie's pay packet never seemed to
increase. Times were tight in the business world, with
non-essential services being cut, and Vanessa had recently lost a couple of regular clients.

'You never call in sick and you're never late. I always
know that I can rely on you and that's rare,' her boss
had told her warmly. 'If we can get more work out of
this contract I'll up your pay…I promise.'

Although Rosie was used to such promises being
broken by Vanessa, she had smiled appreciatively out of
politeness. She was a cleaner because the hours suited
and allowed her to study during the day, not because she
enjoyed it. She also could have told Vanessa some very
practical ways in which she could improve her business
prospects. Well aware, though, that the advice would
be resented, she said nothing when she saw lazy co-
workers being retained and slapdash work done through
lack of adequate supervision. Vanessa was great at jug-
gling figures and seeking out new clients, but she was
a poor manager, who rarely emerged from behind her
desk. That was the real reason why her business was
struggling to survive.

But then, Rosie had long since learned that you
couldn't change people. After all, she had tried for a

long time to change her mother, had encouraged, supported, advised, even pleaded, and in the end it had all come to nothing because, regardless of what Rosie did, her mother had had no desire to change the person she was. You had to accept people as they were, not as you would like them to be, Rosie reflected with a pained sense of regret as she recalled that hard lesson. She remembered countless supervised sessions with her mother during which she had tried to shine bright enough to interest her parent in being a parent and in *wanting* to raise her own daughter. And now she winced, looking back at all that wasted energy and angst, for Jenny Gray had been infinitely fonder of booze, bad boys and a lively social life than she had ever been of the daughter she had purposely conceived.

'I thought your father would marry me—I thought I'd be set up for life,' her mother had once confided on the subject of Rosie's conception. 'He came from a rich family but he was a waste of space.'

As she was nothing like the ambitious fantasist her late mother had been, Rosie privately thought that a lot of men were a waste of space and that women were better company. The men she had dated had been boringly obsessed with sex, sport and beer. As she had no interest in any of that and better things to do with her few hours of free time, it had been many months since she had even had a date. Not that she was ever likely to be bowled over by a rush of male interest in her essentially unexciting self, Rosie conceded ruefully. Rosie was barely five feet tall and flat as a board back and front, embarrassingly bereft of the womanly curves that attracted the opposite sex. For years she had hoped that she was simply a 'late developer' and that if she waited long enough the required badges of woman-hood would magically arrive and transform her body and her prospects, but here she was, twenty-three years old and still downright skinny and ultra-small every-where it counted.

As a straying strand of pale hair brushed her cheek-bone she reached up to tighten the band on her ponytail and groaned out loud when it snapped, digging with-out success through the pockets of her overall in search of a replacement. Her long, wavy hair tumbled round her in an irritating curtain and she wondered for the hundredth time why she didn't just get it cut short for convenience. But then she *did* know why: her foster mother, Beryl, had often told her she had very pretty hair and had liked to brush it for her when she was a child. Sadness momentarily touched Rosie for, although it had been three years since Beryl had died, Rosie still very much missed the older woman's warm common sense and affection. Beryl had been much more of a mother to Rosie than her birth parent.

Alexius sat in an unfamiliar office that belonged to one of his personal assistants, trying to get on with some work, but irritation tinged him every time he reached for something that wasn't on the desk, for it was a discom-fort he was not accustomed to meeting in life. Socrates, he thought grimly of his manipulative godfather, who had played on his conscience to force him into this ju-venile masquerade. His even white teeth gritted as he heard the sound of a vacuum cleaner whirring some-where on the same floor. At least the cleaners had fi-nally arrived and the game could commence. *Game?* Some game! In fact, he felt infuriatingly and uncharacteristically on edge because deception wasn't his style. Yet how could he ever get to know a cleaning operative in the guise of who he truly was? It was only sensible to pretend to be a more humble member of staff, but in doing that he was also making the assumption that Rosie Gray wouldn't recognise him as Alexius Stavroulakis. He doubted that she read the *Financial Times*, where he was regularly depicted, but there was a chance that she was a fan of the celebrity magazines between whose pages he had also made occasional appearances. The more he thought of the deception involved, the more he thought that accidentally bumping into her in some way outside working hours might have been a wiser approach.

Rosie worked steadily down the line of offices, taking care of routine tasks while Zoe took care of the other side of the corridor. Only one office was occupied and the door stood open. She hated trying to clean round employees working late but couldn't risk omitting that room in case checks were made on the standard of their work. Most daytime staff had gone home by eight in the evening and she had to ensure that the schedule of duties laid out for STA was completed right down to the last letter on the contract. She peered into the occupied office and saw a big guy with black hair working at a laptop. Only the Anglepoise lamp beside him was lit, casting light and shadow over his strong, dark features. He glanced up suddenly, startling her, revealing ice-grey eyes as bright as liquid mercury in his lean bronzed face. He was drop-dead gorgeous: that was her first thought and a very uncommon one for Rosie.

Alexius stared, both recognising and not recognising his quarry. Bleached of colour, Rosie Gray had looked so flat and uninspiring in that black and white photograph, but in the flesh she was glowing and unusual… and *tiny*. The Seferis family were kind of small in stature, he recalled abstractedly, but she was as ridiculously tiny and fragile in appearance as a fairy-tale elf. But if her diminutive size almost made him smile, her face and hair riveted him. He had never seen natural hair that colour, a glorious wavy fall as pale a blonde as frost sparkling on snow. It was dyed—of course it was, he assumed, his attention lingering longer still on that amazingly vivid little triangular face of hers: big ocean-green eyes, a neat little nose and a mouth made for sin with the sort of lush pouting outline that gave a man erotic fantasies. Or the sort of man who *did* erotic fantasies, Alexius adjusted, for he did not. When every woman he ever approached was immediately available, there was no need for fantasies. But those succulent pink lips were definitely sexy, although that was not a thought he wanted to have around his godfather's long-lost granddaughter. The oddity of the situation was responsible, he decided impatiently. It was throwing him off-balance.

Colliding unexpectedly with those piercing light eyes enhanced by black curling lashes, Rosie swallowed hard and felt her heart hammer behind her breastbone as though she were trapped. He was so very, very good-looking, from the stark lines of his high cheekbones and the bold slash of his nose to the hard angular jaw line and beautifully moulded sensual mouth. But she was quick to recognise the impatience etched in the twist of that firm upper lip and she hastily withdrew from the threshold to vanish back down the corridor. Alarm bells had rung loudly inside her head: this was not a man she wanted to interrupt or inconvenience.

She would vacuum the big conference room and then return to see if he had gone.

Her disappearance made Alexius bite back a groan of exasperation. As a male used to women going to often ridiculous lengths to attract and hold his attention, he had virtually no experience of pursuing one. But had he really expected a cleaner to walk up to him and start chatting? Naturally, she had gone into retreat. He strode to the doorway, long powerful legs eating up the distance, and his keen gaze narrowed on the small figure trundling a vacuum cleaner.

'I won't be here much longer,' he said, his deep voice sounding unnaturally loud in the silence of the almost empty office suite.

Taken aback by the announcement, Rosie spun round, her pale hair flying across her face, green eyes openly apprehensive. 'I can do the conference room first—'

'You're new, aren't you?' Alexius remarked, wondering what it was about those eyes, that face, that kept him staring longer than he should have done and continually drew his attention back to her.

'Yes…this is our first shift here,' she murmured so low he had to stretch to hear her. 'We want to do a good job.'

'I'm sure you will.' Alexius watched her deal with a vacuum cleaner almost as tall as she was and considerably bulkier and he experienced a sudden crazy need to snatch it out of her small hands and force her to give him her full attention. What the hell was the matter with him? He studied her afresh and registered in shock that he was aroused. It had been a very long time since a sexual response that undisciplined had assailed

Alexius. *Diavelos*, he was no longer a boy, horny in the radius of any attractive female. He didn't understand it, he really didn't understand the effect she was having on him at all because it was outside his experience. She was little and cute and he didn't go for little and cute. He liked tall, shapely women with dark hair and almost never deviated from the type. In many ways outside the business world he was very much a creature of habit, unwilling to compromise, distrustful of anything new or different. His upbringing had taught him to be like that, encasing him in a protective shell of reserve, cynicism and objectivity. He had learned too young that to many people his immense wealth marked him out only as a potential source of profit, a literal target to be impressed, flattered, ultimately used and deceived by the ambitious and the greedy.

It was close to the end of her shift when Rosie finally found the occupied office empty. It was true that the light still burned and the laptop still sat open on the desk, but she was tired and she knew she wouldn't get a better opportunity to finish on time. She was engaged in swiftly whisking a duster over what she could reach of the desk when he reappeared and she froze, intimidated by the size of him filling the doorway. So tall, so dark, so very handsome. And those astonishingly light eyes of his gleamed like polished silver in his strong face.

'I'll move this out of your way,' Alexius breathed, scooping up the laptop, standing so close for an instant that the scent of him enveloped her: the smell of clean, warm male laced with a mouth-watering hint of some exotic cologne.

'No need…I can work around you if you'll just put up with me for another f-five minutes,' Rosie replied a little shakily, her cheeks hot with the awareness of her recent thoughts.

Struggling to run through a mental checklist of small tasks to be done before she could consider her work complete, Rosie noticed the photo on the desk of a pretty blonde woman hugging two young children. 'Nice kids,' she muttered into the awkward silence.

'Not mine. I share this office,' he informed her abruptly, his slight but definable foreign accent obvious as she unfurled the vacuum cleaner for action.

Rosie glanced at him in surprise, for he didn't look the type of male likely to take to *sharing* anything, although she had no idea where she had got that impression from. Perhaps it was something to do with the fact that he had as much physical presence as a ruddy great rock set in her path, not to mention an aura of command and arrogance that had suggested to her that he could be more than just another office drone, earning his daily bread by whatever means were within his power. Hot desking, wasn't that what the practice of sharing desk space was called?

'I'm Alex, by the way,' he murmured smoothly. 'Alex Kolovos…'

'Nice to meet you,' Rosie responded in even greater discomfiture, wondering why he was speaking to her in the first place, because it was certainly not the norm. Men usually only spoke if the cleaner was old enough to remind them of their mother or granny or if they were making a play for you. Zoe, christened by her fellow cleaners 'the Bombshell', had enjoyed several such approaches from men attracted by her pretty face and stunning curves, but no man had yet come on to Rosie during working hours. Was it the fact that her hair was loose? Irritated by the sudden wash of stupid thoughts that had taken over her normally logical brain and ill at ease in his company, she switched on the vacuum, engulfing them both in noise. With secret amusement she watched him wince as if she had scraped a chalk down a blackboard.

'Thanks,' she breezed as she gratefully switched the vacuum off again and sped from the room without a backward glance.

Alexius reflected that it was a humbling experience to chat to a woman without the aura of his billions enhancing him with a wondrous golden glow of magnetic attraction. It had not escaped his notice either that she couldn't wait to get away from him. Was she shy? Or simply wary? Alexius had no experience whatsoever of either female trait and no desire to remedy his ignorance in that field either. He checked his watch: he had a business dinner to attend. Flipping shut his laptop with relief, he stood up to leave. She was extraordinarily sexy, he reflected grimly, hot enough to make him hard as a rock, not at all what he had expected.

Rosie went home that night to be greeted by Baskerville's ecstatic barks and leaps in the tiny lounge off the kitchen that all the women used. Bas was a four-year-old chihuahua. He had belonged to Rosie's foster mother, Beryl, and since Rosie had moved in he had become the house pet, moving freely between the occupants, being spoiled and looked after by whoever was at home. That was a relief for Rosie, who had worried about him getting lonely when she was out and about. Bas tucked securely under one arm, Rosie made herself a plate of cheese on toast and sat down to watch TV and chat with her housemates while she ate and Bas snacked on the crusts and anything else on offer.

At some stage of the night she wakened with pains in her stomach and she was violently ill. In the morning she felt better but washed out.

That evening when she started her cleaning shift, she was tired. Alex Kolovos's office was lit up but he wasn't there. Assuming he would return and stifling a totally pathetic pang of disappointment over his absence, she headed for the conference room instead. The instant she stepped into the room, however, she realised it was occupied because the first thing she heard was his unforgettable drawl. Instantly, she fell still to glance across the long meeting table and butterflies kicked off in her tummy in the most schoolgirlish way as her gaze locked to his powerful figure, where he stood by the window. Her eyes travelled up to his handsome face and a jolt of recognition and pleasure ran through her like an electric shock, her heart rate speeding up, every cell in her body awakening to awareness. In the midst of questioning why the precise arrangement of his features should have that astonishing effect on her, she stopped wondering and just found herself staring while heat and breathlessness assailed her. He was talking on the phone in a foreign language. A couple of familiar words caught her attention as she began automatically to withdraw from the room again: unless she was very much mistaken he was talking in Greek.

Moving an imperious hand to halt her retreat, Alexius studied her, noting that the gorgeous hair was tied circumspectly back and that she still wore no make-up that he could see. The mystery of her appeal, however, was utterly overpowered by the stirring reaction at his groin. One look at that vibrant little face and he wanted to *taste* that luscious pink mouth, to *touch* that delicate little body and discover its every secret. He wanted to sink deep into her, watch her eyes widen in sensual shock and ride her into oblivion. He hadn't felt as hot for a woman since he was a teenager and just as suddenly he was done questioning and was instead enjoying the novelty of the sensation. Last night he had dreamt about her, had actually wakened sweating and hard, and any woman capable of rousing him to that extent was worthy of his full attention. It didn't matter who or what she was any more, it was more a matter of what *she* could make *him* feel. When it came to women Alexius's biggest problem was boredom.

'I'm done here,' he said succinctly, putting away his mobile phone and striding towards her.

'If you're s-sure,' Rosie heard herself stammer slightly, her mouth dry, her eyes pools of deep green, awareness fingering up and down her spine in an embarrassing wave that burned into her cheeks.

'Of course, I'm sure,' Alexius fielded a touch drily, moving past her, noting that her eyes were starry bright and catching a faint whiff of a floral scent that flared his nostrils. He knew at that moment with a triumph he could taste that the attraction wasn't one-sided. Socrates had set him a challenge and he intended to deliver in record time. He would get to know Rosie Gray in every way there was and hopefully he wouldn't have to waste much more time hanging about the office after hours.

Still all of a quiver, Rosie cleaned the conference room and got her breathing back under control. Alex Kolovos hit her a little like a wave, knocking her off her feet and leaving her to struggle for normality in the aftermath. It *was* schoolgirlish to react that powerfully to a man, she told herself in exasperation, but possibly she was overdue for the experience. After all, she was twenty-three years old and still a virgin. When she had been a teenager, her social life had been severely restricted by the fact that she had had to leave school to become her foster mother's carer during Beryl's terminal illness. Opportunities to explore her sexuality had been non-existent and by the time she had regained her freedom, she had become much more cautious and sensible. Until now, though, no man had ever made Rosie's heart pound. Times without number her mother had told her about such wildfire attractions and now, finally feeling what her wayward, self-destructive mother had described, Rosie was torn between fear that she was being very foolish and satisfaction that she could feel what other women felt.

'I've met a man...' Jenny Gray used to confide excitedly when Rosie was a child. 'Someone *special*,' she would savour. 'I'll be away a while.'

And Rosie's mother had often vanished for days on end, leaving Rosie alone in their apartment without heating, money, food in the fridge or clean clothes. It was even worse, though, when she brought the men home, telling Rosie not to come out of her bedroom, lying in her bed or the living room drinking all day and laughing loudly, forgetting that Rosie had to be taken to school and fed and washed. In the end Social Services had removed Rosie and put her in foster care. Rosie's memories were always sobering.

By the time Rosie had finished cleaning every other office, Alex Kolovos was still behind his desk. Taut with wariness, she entered. 'Do you mind if I clean?'

'Not at all,' he said lightly, glancing up from his laptop to smile at her, a smile that carried so much sensual charisma that she felt heat blossom in her belly like a fire being stoked. Only that fire didn't need to be stoked, she thought guiltily, insanely aware of the tautness of her nipples and the shakiness of her legs.

'Would you like a drink?' he enquired, standing in front of a drinks cabinet with a glass in his hand.

Taken aback by the offer, Rosie said, 'No, thanks,' and scolded herself for wanting to say yes. She valued her job too much to flirt on company time and suddenly asked herself what on earth she was playing at. A guy of Alex's ilk wasn't going to offer her anything more than a one-night stand. She wasn't in his league socially or even educationally. While she might be working to make good on the exams she had missed out on through having to leave school early, she guessed that he was probably a graduate.

Irritated by her immediate refusal of a drink, Alexius wondered if he should have offered her dinner instead. It did not escape his notice that she seemed uncomfortable and that, refusing to look back at him again, she removed herself from his office as soon as she decently could. Did she appreciate how much her unavailability added to her pulling power? The prospect of yet another night at the office set his even white teeth on edge.

She should be avoiding him, a sensible little voice murmured in Rosie's head. Anything else was asking for trouble and Rosie had never asked for trouble in her life. Alex Kolovos was like a fever in her blood, upsetting her stability, making her act silly, and the sooner the fire was put out, the better.

With that conviction firmly in mind, Rosie decided

to ask Zoe to clean his side of the office corridor the following evening. Zoe frowned. 'Why?' she asked baldly.

'That guy who's always working late is sort of… flirting with me,' Rosie admitted reluctantly. 'And it's making me uncomfortable.'

'He's welcome to flirt with me any time he likes!' her co-worker confided. 'He's drop-dead gorgeous… you are blind sometimes to your opportunities, Rosie. Don't you fancy him?'

'Yes, but I know it wouldn't go anywhere.'

'Some of the best experiences don't go anywhere but I still wouldn't miss out on them,' Zoe responded with the amusement of a much more experienced woman.

As they packed up at the end of their shift, Rosie having strenuously resisted the desire to look into Alex's office even once, Zoe frowned at her. 'You had me hoping that guy was going to chat me up—chance would be a fine thing! He didn't even look at me…it was like I was invisible. Obviously, it's you that revs his engine.'

Rosie lay in bed that night trying not to be secretly glad that Alex Kolovos had failed to take the bait with Zoe. Zoe was very attractive and she wouldn't have said no to a drink. In fact, Zoe mightn't have said no to a great number of things. Was that what the gorgeous dark Greek had been hoping for? she wondered wryly. A spot of after-hours sex with no strings attached? What else?

'You stick to your usual routine tonight,' Zoe told Rosie before they even started their shift the next night. 'If tall, dark and very handsome annoys you, stand up for yourself and tell him so. I never took you for a shrinking violet, Rosie.'

Her cheeks burning from the sting of that reproof,

Rosie worked faster than usual. It was a Friday night and she would not be back in the building until Monday evening. She passed by Alex's office, saw his proud dark head lift, turned her face away again, determined not to stare. But, oh, *how* she wanted to!

Alexius tracked her down to the staff kitchen where he had seen her co-worker having a cup of tea the night before. It was eight. He was fed up with hanging round the office and exasperated by her avoidance of him. He was even wondering if she had some sixth sense protecting her, warning her that he was not to be trusted. She was right. He had deliberately left a wad of banknotes lying on the carpet below the desk he was using. It was a crude test of her honesty but the best he could come up with at short notice.

'How's the work going?' Alexius enquired lazily, seeing her perched on a stool clutching a mug.

Consternation at his sudden appearance almost made Rosie drop her mug. He seemed to tower over her like a storm cloud, making her more than usually aware of her small build. Her hand shook slightly and tea slopped out, staining her tunic.

'Be careful,' Alexius instructed, lifting the mug from her and setting it safely aside, extending the kitchen roll on the counter to her.

'You startled me!' Rosie tore off a sheet and dabbed her tunic dry.

'I'm sorry,' he murmured, bright mercury eyes locked to her evasive gaze.

Rosie reddened. She was trying *so* hard not to look at that handsome face, but she could visualise him accurately even when he wasn't physically present. 'Do you work late every night?' she asked to fill the buzzing silence.

'Most nights,' he admitted truthfully.

'I suppose you get overtime,' Rosie assumed, colliding with his intent gaze, marvelling at the length of his black eyelashes while feeling an arrow of wicked heat pierce low in her pelvis. 'Either that or you're overworked—'

'I'm a workaholic,' Alexius imparted, studying her moist pink mouth, resisting the urge to reach out, touch it with his own, learn if she tasted as good as she looked. His powerful physique was rigid with self-discipline, the line of his jaw hard.

'Oh…' Rosie reached for her tea again and sipped, limpid green eyes trained on his lean bronzed visage, loving the angular masculine contours at cheekbone and brow before suddenly recollecting herself and sliding off the stool as if she had been burnt. 'I'd better get back to work,' she told him abruptly and brushed straight past him. Seconds later he heard the floor polisher switching on again.

Taken aback by her abrupt departure, Alexius swore softly beneath his breath. She was too wary to take the bait and respond to him. Someone had hurt her, possibly even abused her. His mouth tightened. But what did that have to do with him? Why should he care? If she took the money from below the desk, he would never see her again.

Grateful Alex Kolovos had not returned to the office he used, Rosie got stuck into cleaning it, working faster than her usual pace, eager to get home and start the weekend. She had coursework to complete but, other than that, she was free.

Something jammed in the vacuum cleaner and she groaned out loud, switching it off and getting down on her knees to investigate. She couldn't believe it when she saw a fifty pound banknote entangled and the edge of what appeared to be another. She had to return to the trolley to get a screwdriver and open up the vacuum cleaner to extract the crushed remains of what looked like an enormous sum of money. By then she was filthy with dust and cross as tacks. Where on earth had the banknotes come from? She couldn't just leave them lying on the desk. Brushing herself down and furious that someone could have been so careless with their cash when there was every chance that the cleaners could be blamed for the disappearance of the money, she stood up and hoped that Alexius had not yet left the office. She stalked down to the conference room that she had seen him use before when he was making phone calls and entered, relieved for once to see him lounging back against the table as he talked to someone on the phone.

'Is this yours?' Rosie demanded, tossing the roll of banknotes—now a little ragged round the edges—down on the polished surface of the table. 'It must've been on the floor. It got stuck in the vacuum cleaner—it might have broken it! It certainly won't have done it any good,' she condemned sharply.

Alexius almost laughed out loud at her annoyance. She was fizzing with rage, all five tiny feet of her, green eyes glittering like gemstones in her defensive little face. 'It's mine. Thank you,' he said quietly.

'Don't be so careless!' she told him thinly. 'If that money had gone missing, the cleaners might have been accused of theft!'

'Your honesty does you proud,' Alexius asserted

softly, thinking that he could surely now with good conscience tell Socrates to go ahead and pursue the acquaintance.

'That is *so* patronising!' Rosie shot back at him furiously, amazed at the amount of anger bubbling up through her in response to his insouciant attitude to the situation that might have developed had she not found and returned the money he had misplaced. 'I may be poor but that doesn't mean I'm more likely to be dishonest! You're very prejudiced! There are thieves in every walk of life.'

Far from amused by the cleaner deciding that she had the right to shout at him, Alexius surveyed her with eyes suddenly as cold and wintry as black ice. 'You've had your say and I respect your honesty, even if I didn't like your mode of delivery. Now…*leave*,' he commanded. 'I have calls to make.'

Rosie was stunned by the transformation in him and incredulous that she could have lost control to the extent of raising her voice and being unnecessarily rude. She turned on her heel, thought about apologising and decided that it would be a waste of time as she recalled that chilly look of detachment and enormous authority in his searing gaze. It was as if he had just frozen in front of her into someone else. She had crossed boundaries she should have respected and offended him. She was relieved that she had finished her shift because she literally couldn't wait to get out of the building.

'Are you sure that you don't mind me taking the van home with me tonight?' Zoe pressed as the two women pushed the trolley through the ground-floor foyer.

'No, as I said earlier, I'll catch a bus,' Rosie responded absently.

'Thanks, Rosie,' her dark-haired companion remarked as the two women loaded the cleaning equipment into the back of the van. 'Mum hasn't seen her sister in ages and I'll be able to drop her off early tomorrow and pick her up again on Sunday afternoon.'

'Vanessa never minds as long as you get the van back in time for Monday,' Rosie warned her co-worker as the brunette closed up the van and climbed into the driver's seat.

'Why are you so quiet?' Zoe asked suddenly. 'Did something happen tonight between you and that guy?'

'Nothing,' Rosie lied as lightly as she could.

And it *was* nothing, she told herself. She had met a guy who attracted her to an unbearable degree but nothing had happened and that was as it should be. Ships that passed and all that, better that than a messy collision such as her mother had specialised in. But she could still see him back in that conference room studying her as if she were a particularly repulsive beetle below a microscope, something utterly beneath him, his distaste and antipathy palpable. That had hurt, that had driven deep. She had shouted and he had taken offence and she couldn't blame him for that, could she? She had found his money and he had thanked her for her honesty. What more could he have done? She shrugged off the feeling that a dark cloud had fallen over her.

CHAPTER TWO

ROSIE was walking towards the bus stop when a large bulky shape stepped out of the shadows cast by the tall office block into her path. 'Rosie? I've been waiting for you for ages,' he complained.

What little was left of Rosie's earlier good mood sank like a stone. It was Jason, her former flatmate Mel's boyfriend. Blond and blue-eyed, he had the large square physique of a keen body-builder and his sheer width gave him an undeniable air of menace. She was annoyed that he had the nerve to approach her when she had already made her lack of interest plain. As she thrust up her chin in challenge a surprisingly fierce light brightened her eyes. 'What are you doing here? Why would you be waiting for me?' she asked accusingly.

'Because I wanted to see you, *talk* to you…that's all,' Jason told her, his formidable jaw set at a bullish angle.

'But I don't want to talk to you,' Rosie responded tartly and attempted to walk on past him.

Jason closed a hand the size of a giant meat hook round her forearm to hold her fast. 'I deserve a chance to talk to you—'

'Why the heck would you think that you deserve anything?' Rosie demanded in angry rebuttal, her temper rising at his stubborn persistence. She was tired and fed up and well aware that she had an early start the next morning. The last thing she needed in the mood she was in was to be confronted by the man who had already caused considerable trouble in her private life. 'Thanks to your selfishness, I lost my friendship with Mel *and* my home!'

'Mel and I have broken up. I'm a free man again,' Jason informed her smugly. 'That's why I'm here.'

'I'm not interested… Let go of me, Jason!' Rosie exclaimed impatiently as she attempted to yank herself free of his confining hold.

'Simmer down, Rosie. As I said, all I want to do is have a little chat with you—'

'Let go of me!' Rosie shouted at him furiously, outraged that he was still holding her against her will. *'Right now!'*

'Let go of her.' The intervention came without warning, couched in quiet but surprisingly carrying tones.

Jason flipped round, dragging Rosie with him, the hand he had clasped to her arm tightening painfully. 'What the hell's it got to do with you?' he demanded pugnaciously.

Rosie stared in disconcertion at Alex Kolovos. He must have seen what was happening as he was leaving the building. Jason's face was livid, his stance openly threatening.

'Let go of Rosie,' Alexius instructed curtly, his face hard as granite in the street light.

'Don't get involved in this,' Rosie urged, trying once again to pull free of Jason's grip.

Although coming to the rescue of a damsel in distress was not his style, Alexius experienced not an ounce of hesitation. He had seen the encounter as he emerged from the building and had known that he had to intervene. She was clearly in trouble.

'Yeah, that's right…don't get involved or you'll be sorry!' Jason shouted in a rising rage, at the sound of which Rosie paled and shivered in the cool night air. 'This is a private conversation—'

'Not when you're manhandling a woman,' Alexius interrupted in a tone of undisguised condemnation.

Rigid with raging tension, Jason swore and took a violent swing at Alexius. A gasp of dismay escaped Rosie but, faster than she would have believed possible, Alexius ducked the incoming fist and punched Jason squarely in the solar plexus. Winded, Jason reeled back a step in shock at the hit and thrust Rosie away from him with a brutal shove so that he could more easily move in to attack again. As Rosie lost her footing and went flying across the pavement with bruising force a cry of pain was wrenched from her lips. Almost simultaneously, she heard a shout, Jason's roar of fury and finally the sound of running feet.

In the space of a minute, Alex Kolovos was bending over her and raising her up. 'Don't try to move,' he urged, already noting the blood that had seeped through the legs of her cotton uniform trousers on which she had gone skidding across the pavement. 'Something might be broken.'

'Don't think so…it just hurts,' Rosie was suddenly painfully conscious of the ache of her bruises and the sting of the abrasions inflicted on her legs and arms. She grimaced, feeling ridiculously like a child who had fallen down, reckoning that the skinned knees and elbows she could feel had borne the brunt of the damage.

He was talking urgently in Greek into a mobile phone and her brow furrowed in discomfiture until he switched back to English. 'I'm taking you to a doctor.'

Instantly, Rosie tried to sit up on her own. 'That's not necessary—'

But the sudden movement made her head swim and she felt horribly queasy and just as fast she rested back again on the strength of his supporting arm while struggling to master her body's unfamiliar weakness. She thought she would die of shame if she threw up in front of him.

'What happened?'

'Having met more resistance than he had bargained on, your assailant ran off. You will have to make a complaint against him with the police.'

'I don't want to call the police about Jason,' Rosie said, knowing that she didn't want the fuss or the complications of getting the law involved but, beneath it, helplessly concerned that Jason might make another attempt to corner her when she was alone. What the heck did Jason want from her?

A car drew up beside them. Alexius vaulted upright as the driver jumped out to yank open the rear door. Alexius crouched down to lift Rosie and was shocked by how very little she weighed in his arms, deciding that below the concealment of her clothes she had to be pure skin and bone. He fed her slender body carefully into the back seat of the car so that she could continue to lie down. He climbed in beside her. The door closed. The car moved off.

Still fighting the queasiness in her stomach, Rosie glanced at Alex Kolovos, only to discover that he was frowning down at her. Light eyes bright as stars in his taut, darkly handsome face surveyed her with none of the chill that had confounded her in the conference room, and a flock of butterflies was unleashed in the pit of her stomach. When he looked at her like that, she found him irresistible and the reaction unnerved her. She was terrified that she was behaving like a teenager with a bad crush; her gaze skimmed off him to examine the interior of the car in which she lay. 'Whose car is this? Who's driving?' she asked in dismay.

'It's my car. One of the security guards brought it and offered to drive so that I could keep an eye on you.'

'If you're so convinced that I need to see a doctor why didn't you call an ambulance?' she prompted curiously.

'I knew this would be faster and more efficient,' Alexius responded smoothly. 'And you *do* need to see a doctor. You were assaulted.'

Rosie lowered her eyelashes again, feeling too weak and nauseous to fight him. Even if he was no longer freezing her out, he was domineering and she had never liked men of that ilk. Jason's ilk, she labelled ruefully. Her one-time flatmate, Mel, had gloried in what she had seen as Jason's essential masculinity until she saw the downside of his unpredictable moods and rages, not to mention his habit of making passes at other women whenever the notion took him. But it wasn't fair to compare Alex Kolovos to Jason, Rosie thought guiltily. He was virtually a stranger yet he had risked life and limb to free her from Jason, which astounded her, for strangers usually put their own welfare first.

'Did Jason hurt you?' she whispered, wondering what had happened in the struggle that must have taken place after she had gone careening across the pavement.

Alexius rubbed his hard jaw line thoughtfully. 'He got in one blow before I knocked him down. I was on the boxing team at school. I will have a bruise, nothing more…'

'I'm so sorry,' Rosie muttered. 'I didn't know he was going to be waiting for me. I wasn't expecting to ever see him again—'

'Is he your ex-boyfriend?'

'My goodness, no! I would never get involved with someone like him. He was dating a friend of mine.'

Alexius watched her succulent pink lips compress on that closing remark, which explained nothing. He wondered what the real story was, whether she had encouraged that Neanderthal, who, unless he was very much mistaken, was pumped up both physically and mentally on steroids. He studied her. Her wealth of pale hair was spilling off the edge of the seat in a silken swathe, the big green eyes that dominated her triangular face dark with anxiety. She was still trembling with shock. She was so tiny and vulnerable that he was tempted to put his arms round her to offer comfort. But the very thought of such an unnatural urge shook Alexius to his very depths. When had he ever offered comfort to a woman? Why would he even want to touch her in that way? Sex was one thing and always acceptable, comfort and its complications, something else altogether. It was fitting that he had saved her from further harm and would now ensure that she received medical attention, but there was no need of any more personal element in their dealings. He had already decided to recommend her to her grandfather. While the way she had addressed him earlier had angered him, she was honest and forthright and a hard worker. The next time he saw her she would be in Greece with Socrates. When he had told her to leave, the strangest bad mood had settled over him at the awareness that the masquerade was at an end: he should be rejoicing that the job was done.

The car came to a halt outside a brightly lit town house in an imposing Georgian square. Rosie frowned while Alexius sprang out and turned to scoop her up into his arms before she had the chance to object. 'I can walk!' Rosie protested. 'Where on earth are we? I thought you were taking me to Casualty.'

'Where we would wait for hours before receiving attention. Dmitri Vakros is a doctor and a friend. He is just finishing his evening surgery,' Alex explained.

A nurse greeted Rosie in a small changing room and helped her out of her soiled overalls into a gown. She was ushered into a surgery where a small stocky Greek told her to sit down on the examination couch. He checked her over, frowning at the blackening bruises on her arm from Jason's fingers while the nurse attended to the abrasions on her knees. It all took very little time and she was relieved when she thought of how long she would have had to wait to receive attention at a busy casualty unit where people with much worse injuries would naturally take precedence. Of course, she reflected wryly while she donned her tunic and trousers again, she wouldn't have bothered going to a hospital had she been on her own. Rosie was used to picking herself up from life's more trying events and dusting herself off to go on as normal. Making a fuss or seeking attention had never been encouraged by the social workers who oversaw her childhood. She was secretly amazed that Alex Kolovos had made such a fuss over a minor event, behaving as if she had been badly hurt when she had only suffered the most minor damage at Jason's hands.

'You see, I'm fine,' she told Alex breezily when he sprang upright to greet her in the elegant waiting room. His suit fitted him like a glove, she noted suddenly. It was a dark pinstripe, like something a banker might wear, very conservative, very smart. The close fit accentuated broad shoulders, narrow hips and long, powerful legs. Her cheeks warmed when she realised that she was staring, shaken anew by the obvious dichotomy in their lifestyles.

The doctor emerged from his surgery to talk to Alex and the two men chatted in Greek. It *was* Greek again, which he had been speaking out on the street when he was using his phone, she registered, recognising several words from the classes she had once attended in an effort to learn the language. Throughout the conversation she was conscious of the doctor's frowning curiosity about her and she flushed beneath his assessing gaze. Evidently he was wondering what Alex was doing with a woman dressed as she was, clearly a manual worker and not in the same class as his friend.

'I gather Dr Vakros works in the private sector,' Rosie remarked on the way down the steps.

'Yes.'

'He won't be sending you a bill for seeing me, will he?' Rosie checked worriedly.

'No, our friendship is of long standing.'

'That's a relief. I should be getting on now,' Rosie said rather awkwardly. 'Thanks for all your help.'

'I'm not finished yet—I'm taking you home,' Alex announced, addressing the man already waiting outside the car in Greek and catching the keys that were tossed to him.

'There's really no need for that. I've taken up enough of your evening.'

Alex Kolovos gazed down at her, high aristocratic cheekbones taut, black lashes low over his unnervingly bright eyes. 'I *want* to take you home,' he informed her levelly.

Colour surged into Rosie's cheeks in receipt of that forceful statement. She didn't know what to say, how to react. Why was he putting himself out like this for her benefit? Was he attracted to her or simply a good Samaritan? Why on earth would he be attracted to her? she scolded herself irritably. She was small, flat as a pancake out front where it mattered: men didn't turn their heads to look when she walked by. Embarrassed by her own thoughts and a growing sense of utterly ridiculous inadequacy, she slid into the passenger seat of the saloon car and did up the belt. He drove off but seemed to have difficulty with the gears and cursed only half under his breath when the engine conked out at the traffic lights.

'It's a new car. I haven't driven it much,' he commented in his own defence, cursing the fact that he so rarely drove himself anywhere. From childhood he had had a chauffeur and had only enjoyed the freedom of driving his own car while at university.

Rosie tried not to smile at the excuse. Just about everybody she knew got around the city on public transport. She wondered if his was a company car and if so, did that mean that even though he had to share an office, he was a bigger wheel than she had appreciated in STA Industries? Glancing out of the window, she finally realised that they were travelling in entirely the wrong direction.

'Sorry, I should have given you my address first,' she said and did so.

He hadn't a clue how to get there: that was immediately obvious to her, although he tried to hide it. She gave him directions and tried not to wince as he wrenched at the gears like a learner driver every time they had to stop at traffic lights.

'Will you join me for a meal?' he asked casually when after several wrong turns—she was *lousy* at giving directions—they finally were within minutes of her bedsit.

Surprised by the invitation, Rosie glanced at him in dismay. At the same time her empty tummy emitted an embarrassing growl and she coughed in the hope of masking it. 'A meal?' she prompted.

'By the sound of it you're as hungry as I am,' Alexius remarked, his amusement unhidden.

So, the cough hadn't worked. Rosie reddened yet again. She could not remember ever being so self-conscious in a man's company before and it exasperated her. Circumstances had thrown them together and his was a spontaneous invite. Why not? It wasn't as though he was asking her for a date.

'There's a place just round the corner from my bedsit,' she volunteered. 'It's not fancy but the food's good.'

'That'll do.' Alexius parked the car, noting in the driving mirror that his security team were following in the car behind him. They had probably laughed their socks off every time the car stalled on him, he reflected wryly. But having got into Rosie's good books again, he had every intention of staying on target, even though he knew that he no longer had his godfather as an excuse to spend time with her. He would do as he liked; Alexius *always* did as he liked. When he saw the restaurant, a shabby, brightly lit beacon in a rundown street, he was taken aback. He had never eaten in such a place in his life. The sheer scale of the gulf between their daily lives finally penetrated and disconcerted him. Pretending to be someone else was bringing challenges he had not foreseen.

It was a relief for Rosie to know that she would have no need to cook when she got home. She smothered a yawn as he followed her into the self-service restaurant, popular with shift workers for its long opening hours. She lifted a tray and turned to see Alex scanning his surroundings with wide-eyed attention.

'We serve ourselves?' Alex enquired, a black brow quirking at the concept.

Without fanfare, Rosie handed him a tray and joined the queue. Across the room three women at a table were giving Alex the eye. He seemed quite unaware of their blatant interest as he studied the menu on the wall. He did attract attention though, Rosie conceded, deciding that he was too good-looking for his own good. It was a thought she was familiar with and it had occurred to her the first time she saw a photo of her very handsome blond, blue-eyed father, Troy Seferis. She had always been wary of very attractive men and for the first time it occurred to her that that was a rather unreasonable bias. Alex had waded in to tackle Jason for her sake and she had no reason to think him vain, shallow or self-serving, in fact, the direct opposite. Her green eyes rested on him assessingly. With his black hair, tall, well-built body and that lean, strong-boned face sheathed in bronzed skin, he was extremely eye-catching…and he was with *her*. Her narrow shoulders suddenly straightened and she smiled.

At the checkout Rosie tried to insist on paying for her own meal, which seemed to totally bewilder her companion.

'No woman pays for herself in my company,' he breathed with arrogant finality, passing money literally over her head to conclude the matter.

Rosie gritted her teeth at being overruled. As she grabbed cutlery and a napkin he hovered with his own tray as if he didn't know what to do. As a last resort, she lifted cutlery and a napkin for him and asked him if he wanted water. For a fully grown adult male he could occasionally exude the strangest hint of helplessness, she thought in bewilderment.

'Why didn't you want me to pay for your meal?' he demanded once they had found a table.

'I always pay for myself when I'm with a guy,' Rosie admitted stiffly. 'That way there are no misunderstandings.'

His black curling lashes screened his disconcerted gaze. Socrates was going to like her, oh, yes, Socrates was going to like her a lot, he decided with suppressed amusement. But the concept of a woman paying for herself was entirely foreign to Alexius and he didn't like it at all. 'Tell me about that thug, Jason,' he urged. 'Who is he?'

'Until about ten days ago, I shared a flat with a friend called Melanie. Jason was Mel's boyfriend. One night he grabbed me in the kitchen and tried to kiss me and Mel walked into the middle of it,' Rosie recited, rolling her highly expressive eyes heavenward at the unpleasant memory. 'She blamed me totally for it and said I must've led him on and she told me to get out of the flat. I thought she would have seen sense and cooled down by the next morning but instead she stomped into my room, called me a man-stealing cow and started packing my stuff for me. She threw me out...'

'And Jason?' Alexius watched in fascination as she tucked hungrily into her Irish stew like a woman who hadn't eaten in at least a week. She might be thin but, seemingly, she had a healthy appetite.

'He was forgiven on the spot...or so I assumed, but tonight he said that they've broken up,' Rosie told him wryly. 'Whatever, I still don't want anything to do with him.'

'Bearing in mind his obvious anger management issues, that's wise,' Alexius commented.

'Are you Greek?' she asked suddenly. 'I recognised a couple of the words you used speaking to the guy that drove us to the doctor's.'

He tensed. 'You speak Greek?'

'No, only a few words, tourist stuff,' she proclaimed, her head tilting, pale blonde hair feathering round her cheekbones in artless waves. 'I signed up for classes once but only went to a couple. It's a more difficult language than I expected.'

'Why Greek?' Alexius realised in surprise that he was actually quite content to sit in the dump of a restaurant if it meant he could watch her amazingly animated face, linger on her sparkling eyes and the brightness of her fleeting smiles.

Rosie studied him. He was getting a five o'clock shadow, dark stubble marking his hard angular jaw line and defining his beautifully sculpted mouth. On him, it was an incredibly sexy look. Her tummy turned a somersault inside her as he focused those curiously light eyes on her full force. 'Why Greek? My father was Greek,' she admitted a little shakily, disturbed by the knowledge that he attracted her as if she were iron filings and he were a magnet. That was a scary first for her. 'I never knew him, though. He broke up with my mother before I was born and died soon afterwards.'

'Your mother?'

'She died when I was sixteen—she was diabetic and she wouldn't follow the rules to improve her health and she had a heart attack. I don't have any other relatives. What about you?' Rosie prompted, marvelling that he could be sufficiently interested in her to ask such personal questions, but pleased as well.

'My parents died in a car crash about ten years ago,' Alexius volunteered. 'I was an only child. Aside from a couple of very distant cousins, I'm alone in the world and I prefer it that way.'

Her brow furrowed in surprise. 'But why?'

'Family members can cause you a lot of grief,' he said, his handsome mouth compressing on that clipped judgemental statement.

Rosie reflected that that was certainly true when it came to her own troubled relationship with her mother. Even so, the experience had not soured her entire outlook, but the unyielding angles of Alex's features as he spoke suggested an engrained aversion to such close ties. 'But being a part of a family can also bring great joy and security. It can be a source of strength and comfort. I saw that in one of the foster families I lived with. I've always wanted a family of my own,' she admitted without hesitation.

'Is that why you tried to learn Greek?' Alexius enquired.

'No, I don't have any relatives in Greece either that I know of. But I had this crazy notion that my Greek blood would somehow make the language easier for me to learn.' Rosie pulled a face and laughed at her youthful folly. 'I soon found out my mistake.'

From his side of the table, Alexius was watching her intently. He was trying to work out what it was about her exquisite little face that constantly drew his attention back there. The expressive eyes and the sadness that was there in repose? The delicacy of her bone structure? As she laughed her whole face lit up and reluctant fascination gripped him. She was so natural, so relaxed in his company and he wasn't used to that. She had disagreed with him on the topic of families and had had no fear of saying so and arguing her point. Women, indeed men as well, usually rushed to agree with Alexius while complimenting him on his insight and intelligence. She savoured the dessert she had chosen with tiny spoonfuls, pausing to lick her lips every so often so that not a drop could escape. He stared at that soft full mouth and lust roared through him at breathtaking speed, shocking him back to awareness. For the first time, he wondered if she was deliberately teasing him and if the friendly innocence of her manner was a fake to pull in the unwary.

In the sudden silence that had fallen, Rosie was insanely aware of Alex's intent scrutiny. She could feel every breath she drew, the tightening pulsing sensation in her nipples and the sliding sense of warmth in a place much lower down that she wasn't used to thinking about. An electrifying tension held her still, that treacherous warmth at the heart of her body tugging at her as she stared back at him. She knew it was desire controlling her, knew exactly what it was but could barely believe she was feeling it. The last time a man had got her that hot under the collar she had been sixteen and the object of her affections had been a poster pin-up on her bedroom wall, the lead singer of a long forgotten band. Alex Kolovos was a far more dangerous prospect than that first tender crush.

'It's time I said thank you and went home,' Rosie told him curtly, keen to pull back and make her escape, for she didn't like feelings or reactions that were not in her control. They made her feel unsafe and foolish. It had always been her secret terror that she might have inherited more of her mother's impulsive passionate nature than she had ever appreciated. Jenny Gray had been a pushover for the wrong men, easily impressed, easily bedded, easily discarded. Rosie's mother had lived in a chaos of traumatic relationships, always hoping for something better, never finding it, but hope had sprung eternal with every new man who came along.

Alex sprang upright, lifted her coat from her fingers and held it out for her to put on. 'I'm not used to that kind of attention,' she confided, her face colouring at the admission as they walked out of the restaurant and on down the street. 'You can leave me now. I only live three doors down.'

Alexius said nothing but ignored the invitation to leave. She was unlocking the battered front door when, without even realising it, he put his hand on her arm to stay her. She turned back, colliding with those silvery-grey eyes of his, and her heartbeat hammered so fast she was afraid she might somehow choke on the tightness in her throat.

He wound his hand into her hair and bent his imperious dark head—it was a long way down to her level, he discovered as he captured her lush mouth with his. And that single sweet taste of her went straight to his head like the finest brandy and he kissed her with tortured, driving urgency, hauling her slight body up against him. He wanted her at that moment with a sexual ferocity he had never experienced in his life before.

At his first touch, Rosie had initially frozen in shock, but just as quickly she melted, entrapped by the surge of hunger that leapt inside her like a burning flame that threatened to consume her. Her arms went round his neck without her volition and she rejoiced when he crushed her to him. One little taste of him was only enough to make her crave the next with every fibre of her being. His tongue delved inside her mouth and she gasped, straining into his big powerful frame, desperate to sate the ache in her pelvis as he unleashed a tempest of desire through her body.

As she broke free of him briefly so that she could catch her breath, she was trembling and she didn't want to let him go, didn't want to let him walk away. 'Come in for coffee,' she heard herself say.

Coffee, she thought, trying not to wince as she thrust wide the door. Everyone knew that that was a euphemism for sex, didn't they? What was she doing making such an invitation? Panic almost claimed her. He was more than she could comfortably handle. Her brain told her that she didn't want passion. She didn't want the dreadful feeling of loss clawing at her now as her body longed for him to touch her again. Safety with men meant maintaining a distance, never wanting more than she might receive, ensuring that she didn't feel too much or get hurt. He broke every rule and that was too risky.

Alexius lifted his head, shrewd grey eyes veiled, face tight with self-discipline. What the hell was he doing? What the hell was he playing at here? His body rigid with suppressed arousal, he lowered her back to the ground, knowing that he could more happily have pushed her back against the door and satisfied his hunger there and then. He wanted her. He wanted her more than he had wanted any woman in a very long time. There was nothing wrong with that, he decided abruptly. He didn't need to question his libido.

Determined to see where she lived, he followed her over the threshold. The entrance needed painting and the stair carpet was badly worn. It was dingy and for the first time he thought critically of his godfather, who had clearly committed money to the cause of raising his granddaughter without ensuring that it went to her rather than her mother.

The door to the living room opened and a tiny dog rushed out to leap at Rosie's knees with shrill yelps of joyous welcome. She scooped him up and cuddled him like a toy. Enormous bat ears flexed above big dark eyes and the dog growled the instant he saw Alex. It was a chihuahua but it looked more like a cartoon rat of the nasty variety, Alex decided.

'This is Baskerville… I call him Bas for short—'

'Ah, you got him. He's been fretting for you,' Martha, the older woman in the doorway, declared. 'He knows when you get home and he seemed to know you were late. He's been patrolling that door listening to every sound for the past hour and more. Oh, you've got company…'

'I should've rung you to let you know I'd be late back,' Rosie said apologetically. 'Thanks for looking after Bas.'

'I'll keep him,' Martha declared, smiling and scooping the tiny dog back from Rosie and into her arms. 'He's great company.'

Martha vanished tactfully back into the living room. Rosie hovered. 'Do you want coffee?' she enquired in the rushing silence, barely able to look at Alex, she was so tense, so unsure, but suddenly she knew that she was done with living her whole life in fear, always afraid that she might make her mother's mistakes.

'No, I want you,' Alexius admitted almost harshly, reaching for her again, urging her slight body up against him, crushing that luscious mouth below his again with hungry pleasure.

Rosie let him kiss her because she couldn't stamp out the longing for that kiss or the even more intoxicating one that followed. Desire, she was learning, was a slippery slope. Give way, open the door to a little and you might invite in a whole lot more of the same. His tongue tangled with hers and a ripple of such intense reaction travelled through her that she shivered, hot and cold with sensation, shock and craving, feeling all the things she had never felt before, and, in that weakened state, his every touch was unbearably seductive.

'Where's your room?' Alexius husked, lifting her up in his arms with decisive cool, finally getting her where he wanted her with a fierce sense of satisfaction.

Rosie gave him a conflicted look. 'I don't do this kind of thing, Alex. I don't bring guys home.'

'I'm not just a guy, *moli mou*,' Alexius told her thickly as he mounted the stairs.

'First door on the right,' she told him hesitantly, her heart thumping so hard she was afraid it might stop. 'No, first on the left!'

He claimed her mouth again then with even greater urgency and her body leapt and yearned and learned all at the same time. There was something about him, something that called to her down deep inside. He nudged the door open with his shoulder, brought her down on her narrow single bed and somehow nibbled on the soft sensitive fullness of her lower lip at the same time. His knowing mouth traced the corded delicacy of her throat, touching and teasing places she hadn't known were erogenous to send searing flashes of blinding delicious desire racing through her. She slammed the door shut on the doubts at the back of her head.

CHAPTER THREE

ALEX found the switch of the bedside light and the small room was illuminated, stark and plain and impersonal. Reminding himself that she had only recently moved in, he stared down at her, his lean powerful length taut and pent-up with the hunger she had aroused.

Her glorious hair lay in a tangle across the pillow. There was a dazed look in her soulful eyes. Her mouth was swollen and red from his kisses and the allure of her called to him as strongly as a siren song. He flipped off her shoes, tugged at her sensible socks. He wanted to strip her bare, he wanted to *see* her. Painfully unsure of herself, Rosie came up on her elbows and reached down to unzip her trousers. He brushed her hand away and took over. Was this what men and women did? she wondered, plunged into ridiculous anguish by her own ignorance of how to behave in an intimate situation. Was it the done thing for her to lie there and let him undress her? If the only alternative was for her to get up and strip for him, she could not imagine doing it.

'I don't bite unless you ask me to,' Alexius quipped, enjoying his ability to read her thoughts from her ever-changing expressions while he wondered what might be responsible for her obvious tension at the prospect of sex.

'I'm not very experienced,' she warned him defensively. 'So, don't be expecting too much.'

'I know it will be amazing,' Alexius fielded with a level of assurance that shook her. 'You're a passionate woman.'

'Did you work that out from one kiss?' she teased, scanning the high cheekbones that lent his face such strong, sexy symmetry along with the deep-set mystery of his stunning silvery-grey eyes.

'There were many,' he reminded her. 'No, I see your passion in the way you look at me.'

Instantly, Rosie closed her eyes and he laughed with male appreciation, lightening the moment, putting to flight some of her shyness and uncertainty. 'And how do you look at me?' she traded, lifting fluttering lashes to study him.

'Probably much the same way. The first time I saw you, I couldn't take my eyes off you...'

She remembered him staring: she had been staring too but that statement buoyed her up, restored her flagging confidence. The pull towards him that she felt was not hers alone. In the interim he tugged off her trousers, frowning down at the plasters marring the smooth sweep of her slim, shapely bare legs. There might not be much of her but there was a delicate perfection to every line of her diminutive body, he decided as he roughly unknotted his tie. Rosie came up on her knees, no longer content to be passive, and removed his tie for him. Her hands lowered and slid beneath his suit jacket to his shoulders and the sheer heat of his hard muscular flesh burned through his shirt. She paused, gazing at him eye to eye for the first time, loving the blaze of intensity she saw there. There was nothing cool about Alex in this particular mood and he couldn't hide the fact.

He captured her face between his big hands and claimed her mouth with hungry fervour, his innate need to dominate taking over while a low growl of satisfaction vibrated in his throat.

Her head swam and the tug at the heart of her intensified, so that she leant forward, bracing her weight on his shoulders. She wasn't aware of him unbuttoning her tunic but she absolutely froze in dismay when he slid a hand between the parted edges, her heart thudding like a drum inside her.

She never wore a bra, had never needed to, and this was the moment he would learn that she had nothing much to offer up top where other women had a feminine bounty. But he didn't hesitate or even tense in surprise. Instead, he cupped a slight swell in one hand and stroked a thumb across an almost painfully swollen nipple and she flinched, so on edge that she felt the thrumming power of that casual caress right down to her toes. With his free hand he lowered her down on the bed and straightened to pitch off his jacket, letting it fall carelessly on the floor.

'What's wrong?' Alexius prompted, staring down at her with shrewd questioning eyes as his sure hands curled to the hem of her tunic. 'You're very tense...'

'Could I keep that on?' Rosie heard herself ask plaintively.

'No,' Alexius said simply, drawing her up one-handed to pull it off over her head.

Rosie felt naked, exposed and she didn't like it and

only just resisted the urge to clamp her hands over her flat chest.

'I like your body,' Alexius murmured thickly.

'I don't…'

Ignoring that response with the knowledge that few women appreciated their own bodies, Alexius peeled off his shirt to reveal a truly mesmerising physique, composed of washboard abs and a taut flat stomach peppered by a fine silky furrow of black hair. Rosie's throat closed over. Her mouth ran dry. He was even more gorgeous half-naked than he was clothed. What on earth was he doing with her? Instantly, she suppressed the insecure thought, knowing that she could be her own worst enemy.

He shed his trousers and she looked…*of course*, she looked at the distinctive bulge in his close fitting boxers. It looked massive, and she swallowed hard. From his long, hair-roughened thighs to his broad shoulders and sleek narrow hips, he was all male, lithe and powerfully muscled. As he skimmed off his last garment she glanced hurriedly away, shy and unsure, but when he came back to her she felt his erection brush her thigh and she shivered, thinking, *This is it, I'm a big girl now, time I knew what all the fuss is about.*

'You're cold,' he growled, coming into contact with her nerve-chilled lower limbs, his body hot as a furnace against hers.

He kissed her, and she gripped his shoulders, needing him to hold on to as his tongue mated with hers and the wild fever kicked off inside her again. It was like nothing she had ever felt, an insane, intoxicating flood of need that left her dizzy and trembling. Her hands sank into the silky luxuriance of his black hair. He might wear his hair short but there was a lot of it.

Alexius was struggling to contain his hunger and slow down. She was tiny and fragile and he didn't want to hurt her. Lying there with her eyes wide open and somehow trusting as he gazed down at her, she seemed achingly vulnerable and naive and that sent a chord of dismay travelling through him. And then she shifted under him and her smooth soft skin slid against his and the peachy floral scent of her entrapped him, bringing the desire back full force. With the ease of long habit and strong self-control he stifled the stab of misgiving. She was happy, he was happy, why complicate things? This was sex, nothing but sex, and he never wrapped it up as anything other than a meeting of bodies.

He bent his arrogant dark head and shimmied down a little on the bed to lower his mouth to a very swollen nipple the delicate shade of an apricot and wonderfully ripe. Rosie gritted her teeth as sensation darted through her as though there were a line of elastic jerking taut between breast and pelvis. He rolled the sensitive peaks between his fingers and then he sucked them and her hips rose off the bed and she gasped.

'You like that,' Alexius whispered.

'A lot,' she admitted shakily.

But there was, she discovered, an awful lot more for her to like. There was the slow glide of his fingers along her inner thigh and the unbearable yearning to be touched. A finger sank deep inside and she writhed, breathless with longing. Her tension ratcheted up another notch as he stroked her clitoris, circling, touching, teasing, sending the tormenting pleasure to an ever greater height. The ache between her legs and the desire for more grew steadily.

'*Please...*' she gasped at one stage, not even sure what she was asking for, only knowing that she needed it more than she had ever needed anything.

'Are you protected?' Alexius asked, wishing that he had not tossed his jacket halfway across the room.

Rosie had once suffered from cramps and her doctor had advised her to take the contraceptive pill. She nodded in silence. 'Not stupid,' she squeezed out.

He sank his hands beneath her bottom to lift her to him and his erection nudged her core, seeking entrance. He moved slowly, carefully. 'You're so small, so tight,' he ground out. 'I could almost think you hadn't done this before...'

She parted her lips to confirm the fact but no sound came out because all her concentration was on what was happening to her just then. He was pushing inside her, stretching her and it was the most extraordinary sensation as her body adapted to welcome him. Then with a groan of frustrated hunger he shifted his hips and drove deeper, and the sharp pain as he broke through the barrier of her innocence provoked a sharp cry from her.

'What the hell—?' Alexius demanded rawly although even at that point he was very much afraid that he knew very well what the matter was.

'S'pose I should've warned you,' Rosie mumbled, embarrassed to death by the cry she had given.

Alexius levelled forbidding icy-grey eyes on her flushed and anxious face. 'You're a virgin?'

'Not any more,' she pointed out helplessly. 'My choice, my decision.'

Alexius gritted his teeth in annoyance. The deed was

done. Her choice, *not* his and not a position he was used to finding himself in. But it was the work of a moment to let the dam of hunger he had rigorously restrained flow free and he buried himself deep in the silken welcome of her hot little body.

Her inner muscles clenched round him as tiny little tremors of pleasure began to course through Rosie. She had feared he might stop; she hadn't wanted him to stop. Now he began to move, harder, faster, deeper and the excitement returned with an intensity that took her breath away. Raw sensation and energy controlled her now and she tilted her hips and locked her legs round him in instinctive welcome. The pleasure came in an electrifying wave, tingling and burning through her every fibre, and then it peaked as she came in shock at what she was feeling. Alexius shuddered and poured himself into her, on a high of excitement that was new to him. He looked down at her to see that tears had left glistening trails down her cheeks and knew that she had been overwhelmed as she gazed up at him in astonishment. He released her from his weight and, even though he usually rolled away from his lovers the instant he had achieved satisfaction, he pulled her back into his arms and held her close, his heart thudding madly against hers.

'Are you all right, *moli mou*?' Alexius asked, his breath fanning her cheek. 'Are you in pain?'

'No.' Rosie suppressed her embarrassment by burying her face in a strong brown shoulder, drinking in the hot musky scent of him and loving it. She felt both light as air with happiness and exhausted. 'I'm totally fine, Alex.'

'Is there anywhere I can get a shower here?' Alexius

enquired, suddenly ill at ease with the way he was hold-ing her to him and in search of a good get-out clause. He lacked the cuddle gene and didn't even pay lip-service to it, but her tiny body felt surprisingly good nestled close to him, and he discovered that he was ridicu-lously reluctant to risk hurting her feelings by push-ing her away.

'There's no hot water at this time of night,' she mut-tered uncomfortably. 'I'm sorry.'

'It's not a problem.' It was a lie: the lack of hot water was one more unnecessary reminder that he was in an unfamiliar environment in an unacceptable situation with a woman he should never have touched. He felt disorientatingly like an accident victim while he tried to work out how he, a guy who was very logical and controlled and a terrific planner, could have ended up in such a position. When had the rot set in? The instant he saw her standing in that office doorway? Little and cute, which had never attracted him before, he rumi-nated grimly. She didn't even know *who* he was and she trusted him. That bothered the hell out of him and he didn't even know why. The deep, even tenor of her breathing and the relaxed weight of her against him informed Alexius that she had fallen asleep. He eased one leg out of the bed slowly and quietly while edging Rosie back down, covering her with the duvet. And then he got dressed, swiftly and silently, his face set in forbidding lines.

As he stepped out onto the landing something tugged at his trouser leg and growled. He looked down. Bas had a mouthful of his trousers. He tried to shake him off; it was a mistake. Bas took advantage of the defensive movement to sink his needle-sharp teeth into Alexius's leg instead. Alexius gritted his own teeth in disbelief and then bent down to detach the chihuahua from his flesh. It wasn't easy because Bas fought back, snarling and growling as if under attack. Finally, Alexius had the writhing little body captured in one big hand. Enraged big brown eyes glared at him from below the ridiculous bat ears.

'I deserved it…you're right,' Alexius breathed, gently opening Rosie's door and pushing the tiny dog through the gap before quickly closing it again. Baskerville, she had called the dog. Now what was the name of that Sherlock Holmes story? *The Hound of the Baskervilles?* If the nasty little animal hadn't bitten him, Alexius would have laughed, for Bas, undersized though he was, had lived up to his name.

A bastard, he reflected, would simply tell Socrates that his granddaughter was a bad bet. That way Rosie would be deprived of a fortune and Alexius would never have to see her again or acknowledge what he had done. But having got to know Rosie in the flesh, Alexius knew he couldn't do that. He also knew that, having had her once, he already wanted her again. But he couldn't do *that* either. An ongoing affair with his godfather's grandchild was out of the question. Socrates would expect him to marry her and, while Rosie seemed to fire Alexius's sex drive as no other woman before her, he had no intention of marrying anyone. Sex was literally all he had to offer her and in this particular scenario it wasn't enough.

He walked downstairs and out of the front door. His protection unit, the four-man team who watched over him everywhere he went, was sitting in a car on the other side of the street. He hailed them. He would get back to his own life and within days it would be as if this strange episode with Rosie had never happened, he thought impatiently. He had made a mistake but everyone made mistakes and there was no point in beating himself up over a one-night stand.

Rosie slept in the next morning and had a frantic rush to get to her maths class in time. It was late afternoon before she had the opportunity to consider the fact that Alex had left during the night without even asking for her phone number or leaving her a note. Her discussions with more experienced friends warned her that that was not unusual behaviour. But once it sank in that she had slept with him on what was virtually the first date, her mood plummeted. Even the magazines warned that men were less keen in those circumstances and more inclined to deem the woman concerned *easy* and less desirable. Of course, Alex could be simply assuming that he would see her on Monday evening when he was working late again, she reasoned, frantically keen at the hope of seeing him again on her horizon.

Her spirits rose to a bubbling high when she got home that afternoon to find a gorgeous bunch of flowers awaiting her, the gift card signed only with a large letter, 'A'. He wouldn't have spent that much money if he wasn't planning to see her again, would he? She borrowed a vase from one of her housemates and set it in the cramped lounge where everyone could enjoy the flowers.

But when Rosie arrived for work at STA Industries on Monday evening, the office Alex shared was empty. She thought he might be away on a business trip and refused to fret about it, but as the week crept on without a single glimpse of him the optimism roused by the expensive bouquet began to drain inexorably away. Was it possible that he was simply avoiding her? The suspicion made her cringe in mortification. He was a professional man and he had slept with a humble cleaner. Maybe he was ashamed of the fact.

On the Friday, her boss, Vanessa, phoned to tell her that the following week she would be working somewhere else. The job at STA Industries was finished and she would not be returning there. But although that temporary contract was now at an end, STA Industries had offered Vanessa's cleaning service a more lucrative twelve-month contract at another one of their companies. So that was that, Rosie thought numbly that weekend. She would never see Alex Kolovos again. He had obviously sent her the flowers out of some misplaced sense of guilt while aware that he had no intention of contacting her again.

Wham, bam, thank you, ma'am, she reflected painfully, astonished by how much his rejection hurt and made her question herself. She had taken a risk, had awarded her trust to a man she barely knew and she had suffered accordingly. *Let this be a lesson to you*, she told herself squarely, exasperated by how torn up she felt about the disrespectful way he had treated her. Alex had only wanted to get her into bed and, having achieved that so easily, he had had no desire to repeat the experience. Now that she knew he had gone for good she allowed herself to recall how disconcerted he had been to become her first lover. Clearly an amateur between the sheets had little appeal for him.

At the end of the second week, Rosie was concerned when her period failed to arrive because she was usually as regular as clockwork in that department. She reminded herself that she was on the pill and very unlikely to be pregnant but the fact that she had slept with Alex still loomed large in her mind. One anxious week after that she made an appointment to see her doctor and was sent straight off for a pregnancy test.

'But I'm taking the contraceptive pill—I thought I was protected!' Rosie exclaimed when the doctor broke the news that she had conceived.

The doctor was kind, understanding and he asked her several specific questions, one of which was had she suffered from any stomach upsets. And then she remembered that night she had been ill and her eyes locked with the doctor's in sudden dismay and comprehension.

'You probably threw up your pill and that compromised your protection. You should have taken other precautions for the rest of the month,' he pronounced with a sigh.

Rosie left the surgery in a daze, barely able to believe that what she had been told was true. It didn't seem possible to her that what she had shared so briefly with Alex could result in an actual child, but there was something very realistic about the numerous leaflets on pregnancy that she had had pressed on her at the surgery. A baby, she thought sickly. How on earth would she ever be able to cope with a baby when she could barely afford to feed and clothe herself?

It occurred to her that Alex Kolovos was equally responsible. Why hadn't he used a condom? Why had he relied on her precautions? Why should he get away scot-free in ignorance while her life was plunged into chaos? Bitterness scythed through Rosie. Why did she have to be caught the one and only time she had strayed from the straight and narrow? And what chance did the unfortunate little mite she had conceived so carelessly have of a happy life? Rosie had been planning to go to university in the autumn. She had two offers from good universities conditional on the results of her exams, which she was due to sit in a couple of weeks. She wanted to study business management but how was she going to manage that with a baby in tow?

Alex should be told, Rosie decided unhappily that evening while she cleaned offices in another company belonging to the STA Industries group. He had the right to know: it would be his child as well. No doubt he would be displeased, if not downright annoyed. Rosie could not find it within her heart to feel sorry for him on that score. A child would wreak less havoc on his life than on hers.

The next morning before she could lose her nerve, Rosie caught the tube to the headquarters of STA Industries, got into the lift and travelled up to the top floor. The svelte receptionist viewed her with polite curiosity as she uttered her request to see Alex Kolovos.

'There's no one of that name working here,' the young woman responded drily.

'Oh, there *is*. I met him two...three weeks ago. He worked late a lot,' Rosie specified, her cheeks warming as the receptionist frowned at her. 'I'll sit down and wait while you track him down.'

'I can't track down someone who doesn't exist,' the woman retorted crisply. 'I know every member of staff and there is no one of that name employed here.'

Rosie sank down gingerly on the edge of one of the sleek leather sofas in the luxurious waiting area. She was tense and uncomfortable, conscious that she looked out of place in her jeans and jacket when everyone else, both men and women, wore smart dark suits. Could Alex have lied to her? Given her a false name? My goodness, could that photo on his desk have been his, after all? Was it possible that the man she had slept with was married? Paper-white and sick at that sudden appalling suspicion, Rosie watched the receptionist make a phone call and noticed that she was deliberately not looking in her direction and talking very quietly. Was she the subject of that phone call or was she being paranoid? All of a sudden the woman shot her a startled glance and frowned.

'Someone is coming to help you with your request,' the receptionist announced with perceptible discomfiture.

Had she called building security to have her thrown out? Rosie's face turned red as fire. *Was* Alex married? Had he given her a fake name?

An older man in a suit strode into Reception. 'Miss Gray?'

Rosie stumbled upright. 'Yes? I can show you the office Alex worked in—'

'That will not be necessary, Miss Gray. Er...Alex is waiting to see you,' he informed her. 'Come this way...'

Her smooth brow indenting, Rosie caught the stunned expression on the receptionist's face and wondered what on earth was going on. Had the receptionist lied to her? She pushed a stray strand of pale hair off her hot face and grabbed her bag to follow the older man down a short corridor she had only vacuumed before, for the door at the end led into the big boss's office and it, not having been included in the cleaning schedule, had been kept locked while she had worked there.

'Where are we going?' Rosie prompted tautly.

Without answering her, he thrust open the imposing door. 'Miss Gray, sir.'

Rosie stepped into a huge light-filled office and blinked nervously, the tip of her tongue snaking out to moisten her lower lip as her attention fell on the tall male poised beside the glass desk. Behind her the door closed, welding her into the awful buzzing silence.

'Alex?' she whispered uncertainly.

He stepped out of the sunlight. 'My full name is Alexius Kolovos Stavroulakis,' he drawled. 'In an effort to be discreet I gave you only part of it. Fortunately, Titos, the head of my security team, recognised the name you gave to the receptionist.'

Stavroulakis? Even Rosie knew that the S in STA Industries stood for Stavroulakis. He wasn't an employee, he was the boss and a very wealthy and powerful man, yet he had deliberately misled her as to his identity. In the bemused frame of mind she was in, her tension surged so high as that shock hit home hard and she felt horribly dizzy.

'Stav-vroulakis?' she stammered almost incomprehensibly as she swayed, fighting off the waves of giddiness assailing her and making it impossible to focus on him. 'But why would a guy like you come after a woman like me?'

In the stark daylight she was white as a sheet, her eyes pools of shock and uneasiness. He saw her sway and strode forward, but not fast enough to catch her as she dropped to the floor in a heap with a tiny little moan.

With a presentiment of doom unequalled in his experience, Alexius Kolovos Stavroulakis bent down and lifted her slight body up into his arms. He could think of only one reason why Rosie might have taken the trouble to seek him out and he was very much hoping that he was wrong.

CHAPTER FOUR

ALEXIUS surveyed Rosie where she lay on the sofa in his penthouse apartment. She was coming round again, her slight body shifting, a sigh fleeing her lips. She looked like a doll, a doll dressed as a teenager in jeans, striped sweater and jacket. A woolly hat with a bobble actually stuck out of one jacket pocket. The canvas shoes on her feet were badly worn, the fabric backing showing through in places. *Thee mou*, what the hell had he been thinking of when he bedded her? And the answer was that he had not been *thinking* at all. Finally, he let his attention rove to her delicate profile, the lashes fluttering now, faint pink warming her cheekbones as natural colour drove away the extreme pallor she had worn only minutes earlier. Her soft pink mouth pouted and he hardened in a reaction as predictable as a wave hitting the shore, he decided wrathfully. He could still feel the hot tight embrace of her body, but even better did he recall the look of wonder in her eyes afterwards. No woman had ever treated Alexius to a look quite like that. Indeed, for three long, endless weeks, Alexius had been reliving that night, trying to sleep with an erection that wouldn't quit, dreaming about her, waking up still unsatisfied and still angry with himself.

He had got *involved*, something he never did with a woman, and it looked as if that error of judgement was going to pay off in spades in record time.

Rosie opened her eyes on a great wall of glass that she didn't recognise and sat up in dismay to glimpse a rooftop view of London that could only belong to someone who inhabited a hugely privileged world. Her head swam and she grimaced at the discomfort.

'Don't try to get up while you're still feeling woozy,' Alex advised smoothly.

Not Alex, *Alexius*, she reminded herself doggedly, finally turning her head to look at him. There he was, standing straight and tall, arrogant black head tilted back, and it was a moment when he looked every inch what he was: a very well-dressed rich and powerful businessman with silver eyes as sharp as a laser beam. He was so beautiful it hurt her to look at him and she dropped her gaze again, protecting herself from her weakness. But those lean, darkly handsome features of his were breathtakingly beautiful and she no longer marvelled at the ease with which he had got her into bed. He was uber-temptation, way beyond what an ordinary girl could expect to meet up with and withstand.

'Where am I?' she asked.

'This apartment is above my office. I wanted privacy in which to talk to you.' His voice was concise, cool, measured. His complete calm gave her a horrendously strong desire to slap him.

'You lied to me about who you were.'

It begins, Alexius thought fatalistically. 'I didn't lie. I merely omitted certain portions of the truth.'

Rosie swung her feet to the smooth wooden floor. Her attention skittered across smoked glass tables, lux-

ury furniture and several very impressive paintings and
the dazed feeling she was suffering from returned in
full force. She was a fish out of water in such opulent
surroundings. 'Semantics and I just bet you're a master of them! What the heck kind of a game were you
playing with me?'

'Sit down again, Rosie,' Alexius urged. 'It wasn't a
game. Your grandfather—'

'I don't have a grandfather—'

'Your father's father, Socrates Seferis, is still very
much alive,' he countered.

'My mother told me that my father had no living
relatives,' she replied argumentatively, chin lifting in
challenge.

Even with her hair scraped back in a no-nonsense
ponytail, she was quite astonishingly pretty, Alexius reflected grimly, not best pleased to have noticed the fact.
Quite deliberately he thought of the sort of woman who
usually attracted him. Tall, curvy, dark-haired and ladylike, and here was Rosie, tiny, boyish in shape, quick-
tempered and cheeky and quite irresistibly appealing
on some level he couldn't penetrate.

'Your mother knew very well that your grandfather
existed because she applied to him for financial help
after your father deserted her when she was pregnant
with you,' Alexius told her. 'He gave her money.'

Rosie had paled and slowly she sat down again. 'But
I never saw any money.'

'That may be so. I'm aware that you grew up in foster care but nonetheless the fact remains, your grandfather *did* care about what happened to you and did
what he could to ensure that you were raised in comfort and security.'

Rosie stared at her canvas-shod feet. She had never had security, even at Beryl's house when she was aware that she could be moved on to other carers at any time. But she was now recalling a period in her life when her visits with her mother had been almost exciting. Jenny had had loads of photos to show her daughter of foreign beaches and fancy hotels and she had worn colourful flashy clothes and skyscraper heels. Later, with hind-sight, Rosie had assumed that her mother must've had a rich boyfriend providing her with those luxuries. But what if the money that had financed Jenny's designer wardrobe and frequent travels abroad had come from Rosie's grandfather, Socrates, instead? It was certainly possible that Jenny Gray had lied. If she had accepted money to help her raise the child she was *not* actually raising, it would have been an act of fraud that could have got her mother into serious trouble, Rosie rea-soned ruefully. What was more, even as a child Rosie had realised that her mother commonly told lies when it suited her to do so. It made sense that Jenny would have concealed Socrates's existence to cover her own tracks. Alexius's version of events might well be the truth as Rosie had never known it but what she could not comprehend was why Alexius Stavroulakis should be discussing her unknown grandfather with her.

'What's your place in all this?' Rosie demanded with spirit. 'What connection do you have to my grandfa-ther? How do you know these things about my back-ground?'

'Socrates Seferis is my godfather and a very old friend.' Alexius breathed in deep and slow, relieved that she seemed calm for all the air of bewilderment that clung to her. 'He asked me to get to know you and tell him what you were like.'

'Get to know me?' Rosie repeated, studying him in frank astonishment. 'Why would he do that?'

'He wanted to know what sort of woman you were before he invited you to visit him in Greece and he trusted my judgement. It should interest you to know that I've already informed Socrates that you are every-thing he could hope for in a granddaughter,' he deliv-ered with patronising cool.

'And that's *why* you started talking to me, helped me out with Jason, took me for a meal?' Rosie guessed sickly, her heart sinking down to her sock soles in the strained silence. It had all been a lie, *everything* from his first taking notice of her to his seeming interest and the amazing pleasure he had introduced her to in bed that same evening.

'Naturally the sex wasn't part of the plan,' Alexius remarked with perceptible distaste.

White as milk, whipped by that distaste, Rosie gazed back at him, big green eyes pools of distress and cen-sure. Her small hands balled into defensive fists.

'I took advantage of you when you were vulnerable. That was wrong,' Alexius murmured even though it was a challenge for him to sound suitably humble. He had no intention of apologising for the best sex he'd had in a decade but he was well aware it had been inappropri-ate in the circumstances.

Rosie stared at him through her cloaking lashes, her heart thumping far too fast for comfort. With shame she felt the clamour of her awakened body respond to him, the tightening tingle of her nipples and the surge of damp awareness between her legs. He had taught her to want him and now that deceptive sense of intimate connection was ready to betray her. But he was not the guy she had believed he was: he really was a stranger. She refused to think about him taking advantage of her because that made her feel small and out of control of her own destiny. That was a humiliating appraisal of their intimacy that she just did not need at that moment.

'That cash that supposedly got caught up in the vacuum cleaner? Was that some sort of a test?' Rosie pressed bitterly.

'A rudimentary but effective one. I needed to know for my godfather's sake if you could be trusted,' Alexius declared smoothly. 'Please accept that I did not intend to injure you in any way when I approached you. I was trying to help out a close friend at his request. Have you no questions to ask about your grandfather?'

Picking up on the hint of reproach in that query, Rosie stiffened even more. 'Should I have? A man whom I didn't even know existed until five minutes ago? A man who knew I existed but who has never tried to meet me? And a man who asked you to check me out for him, rather than get to know me himself?'

That was a cooler and more critical appraisal of the situation than he had expected to receive from a woman who had already admitted that she was keen to have a family. Alexius frowned, disappointed by her response. 'There is some excuse for his behaviour. Socrates had major heart surgery only a couple of weeks ago and he is currently recuperating at his home in Athens. He is in no shape to fly over here to meet you in person.'

'I'm sorry to hear that, but since he was so keen to have me vetted behind my back to see if I was the sort of person he was willing to know, I can't say much more,'

Rosie countered curtly. 'I think this is a horrible way to find out that I have a grandfather. You lied to me—'

'I didn't *lie*,' Alexius shot back at her icily. 'My full name is legally Alexius Kolovos Stavroulakis.'

Her triangular face froze as if overnight frost had struck it pale and tight. 'You lied,' she said again. 'You wanted to mislead me as to who you really were and it worked. I was so stupid, I fell for it!'

Alexius stiffened, fiercely resisting an urge to move closer. The distress in her darkened eyes struck him like a slap in the face. 'I'm sorry but I hope you will forgive me when you meet your grandfather—'

'I'm not planning to meet him,' Rosie told him flatly. 'I've got enough trouble in my life without going out on a limb to meet some old man who tried to judge whether or not I was worth knowing before he even met me.'

'Socrates has asked me to bring you to Greece. Don't let the offence I have caused be laid at his door,' he advised grimly. 'If you do, I believe you will live to regret it. You are a kind-hearted woman.'

'Kind-hearted?' Rosie settled blistering green eyes of condemnation on him. 'If you were standing at an open window at this moment I'd push you out of it! I hate you—'

'You hardly know me…how can you hate me?' Alexius fielded drily.

Taken aback by that unwelcome reminder, Rosie stood up and walked across the room, taking in everything around her, recognising that the perfectly decorated walls and toning upholstery were undoubtedly the work of a top-class interior designer. It looked like a glossy magazine spread: faintly unreal. She turned back to collide unexpectedly with stormy liquid-silver eyes. 'Why are you angry with me? What have you got to be angry about?' she demanded furiously.

Alexius, who prided himself on his powers of camouflage and reserve, gritted his even white teeth together. 'I'm angry that I made such a mess of getting to know you that you will take it out on your grandfather.'

'I don't take things out on people who haven't done me any harm. I'm sure he's a nice old man and I wish him well, I truly do,' she muttered uncomfortably. 'But I don't know if I want to meet him and I certainly don't want to go anywhere with you after what I've found out about you!'

'What have you found out about me that is so threatening?' Alexius traded, striving not to notice the pert curve of her derriere in the jeans and the tininess of her waist. He liked her body, the delicacy and restraint of it, the slender perfection that had so entranced him in her bed. The pulse at his groin quickened, and he felt the heavy push of arousal.

'You might as well be an alien from another planet,' Rosie told him truculently, throwing up her hands in expressive comment on the opulent room. 'You're rich and educated. I'm poor and struggling to complete my education. But, worst of all, I can't trust you because you don't tell the truth.'

His shapely sensual mouth quirked with a hint of amusement that infuriated her. 'If it helps, I can promise you now that I will not tell you another half-truth or omit the truth no matter how unwelcome it may be to you.'

'That would be a good start. I mean, how rich are you?' she prompted shakily. 'Do you have a private jet?'

Alexius had a fleet of them but decided to keep that news to himself. He nodded confirmation.

Her face fell in disappointment because she had hoped that he was not *that* rich. 'And do you own more than one house?'

Beginning to appreciate by the expression on her revealing little face that she was not enamoured of what she was finding out about his bank balance, Alexius released his breath in an impatient hiss. 'Yes. I inherited a great deal of money from my parents, both of whom were wealthy in their own right when they married.'

How dumb must she have been to believe that he was a comparatively ordinary guy? Pain gripped Rosie, pain that she could have been so blind as not to notice the very expensive gold wristwatch he wore, the diamond-encrusted cufflink winking against the pristine white of his shirt, the impossibly well-tailored cut of his striking dove-grey business suit. Not an office worker with a company car. No, he owned and ran the business and, according to her employer, STA Industries was an extremely large international concern.

'Why did you come looking for me, Rosie?' Alexius prompted quietly, wondering why it had never occurred to him before that a woman might actually exist who saw his great wealth only as a barrier and a problem. The concept fascinated him.

Rosie rested dulled green eyes on him and shifted a tiny shoulder in a fatalistic shrug. 'Because I'm pregnant...'

And that bold announcement just lay there in a silence that grew and grew until it seemed to fill the whole room and threaten to suffocate her, impelling her back into urgent speech.

'Sorry to dump it on you like that but, although I was taking the contraceptive pill as I told you, I had a stomach upset that same week and my doctor thinks that the sickness probably wrecked the level of my protection,' she extended in a jerky rush.

Alexius continued to study her much as though she had landed in a parachute in front of him without warning. He had lost colour beneath his bronzed complexion and he was very tense, his brilliant eyes veiled, his hard jaw line clearly delineated. 'You're pregnant? Are you sure?'

'Of course, I'm sure. Tests can tell very early these days,' she muttered uneasily.

'And you're sure it's mine?'

'You know there wasn't anyone else before you and I can assure you that there's not been anyone else since,' Rosie proclaimed curtly, resenting that he had asked that question even if logic suggested he had the right to ask it. 'It's your baby.'

A *baby*. The very concept of a baby blitzed Alexius's brain. Adrenalin pounded through him, powering aggression that had no hope of escape because with her words she had fulfilled his worst fear. She had trapped him as he had always sworn he would never be trapped. He had friends who had put themselves in the same position and it hadn't worked out happily for any of them. All his adult life he had been careful not to take that risk and yet with her, for no more reason than the fact that his jacket was lying halfway across the room, he had had sex without adequate precautions. As the more experienced partner, he could only blame himself for accepting that threat of consequences without real thought of what it might mean if things went wrong. And they had gone wrong, *horribly* wrong, he registered harshly.

'You're shocked,' Rosie breathed, stiff with discomfiture at the acknowledgement. 'I was shocked too but I'm afraid I don't want a termination—'

'I wouldn't ask you to have one,' Alexius cut in smoothly. 'We're adults. We will deal with this.'

'Babies aren't so easy to deal with,' Rosie remarked helplessly, thinking of the heavy round-the-clock demands of the babies she had come across in the foster-care system. A baby was almost a full-time job, she thought fearfully. It couldn't be left alone for a minute. It needed constant care and might not even sleep through the night. The birth of a baby would blow her life apart and wreck all her plans for the future.

'I could have done without this right now,' Rosie added ruefully. 'I have my exams to sit in two weeks. I'm in the middle of my revision and now I can't concentrate—'

'You're studying for exams?' Alexius emerged from his black cloud of foreboding to enquire.

'Yes, I want to go to university in the autumn.'

Alexius thought about the giant holes in the investigation Socrates had had done on her. Just as the photo had not shown her beauty, the basic facts, right down to her current address, had been outrageously inaccurate. She was not content simply to clean offices for the rest of her life; clearly, she had drive and ambition and had he asked a few more personal questions he might have discovered that for himself. But in the long run, who she was, *what* she was, no longer mattered in the face of the fact that she had conceived his child. Socrates deserved better than that embarrassment at his hands.

He dragged in a shuddering breath and braced himself to make the ultimate sacrifice of freedom and self-will. 'I'll marry you…'

Rosie laughed and frowned simultaneously as though he had cracked a rather off-colour joke. 'Don't be daft,' she said, staggered by the suggestion.

Alexius gritted his teeth because marriage was the only acceptable solution he could see to the problem, loathe that reality though he did. 'I'm serious. I'll marry you. It will give the baby my name and I will support you so that you do not suffer in any way.'

Belatedly appreciating that he was completely serious in his offer, Rosie stared at him wide-eyed. 'You would do that? You would actually marry me?' she pressed in helpless fascination.

'It is what I should do for your sake…and the child's.' Cool silvery-grey eyes enhanced by startlingly black lashes met hers unflinchingly. 'I cannot leave you to raise my child alone.'

'You're worried about what my grandfather might think,' Rosie assumed. 'But people don't get married now just because there's a baby on the way.'

'It's still the right thing to do,' Alexius responded flatly. 'The most practical approach.'

'I disagree. You don't *want* to marry me, Alex. I wouldn't marry you on that basis. It wouldn't be fair to either of us,' Rosie countered quietly. 'But I suppose I should thank you for asking—it was a nice thought.'

Alexius stared back at her in stunned silence, unable to believe that she was actually turning him down and with the barest minimum of deliberation. 'A "*nice* thought"?'

'You taking the old-fashioned approach even though

it's not what you personally want,' Rosie extended in rueful clarification of her thoughts. 'No, you're quite safe on that score. I don't want to marry you either. Please be honest with me—'

Alexius compressed his handsome mouth hard. 'I *am* being honest, Rosie—'

'Alex, you don't want me as a wife and you don't want to be a father either. I can *feel* that reluctance in you,' Rosie muttered with emphasis, her wide green eyes troubled but open. 'You don't need to pretend otherwise with me. I'm just as shocked as you are about the baby but we don't have to get married to do the right thing.'

'Your grandfather will very much disagree with you.'

'Well, should I ever meet him, we'll have to agree to differ. I don't want a reluctant husband or an unwilling father for my child and that's sensible, not silly,' Rosie pointed out with conviction. 'For a start I couldn't fit into your world. Your friends would laugh at me. I'd embarrass you. I'm a cleaner, for goodness' sake!'

'Nobody would laugh at you while I was around,' Alexius ground out forcefully, his accent thickening his vowel sounds to send a quiver of awareness running down her spine. 'I would make a real effort to be a good husband and father—'

'But you don't love me…and to have you *trying* all the time would be very hard on my self-esteem,' Rosie protested.

Alexius threw her a derisive look that stung. 'Love is lust, nothing more, and I can assure you that in that department I'm unlikely to disappoint you.'

Confronted by that amount of cynicism, Rosie was more than ever convinced that she was making the wisest decision. 'I don't agree that all love between men and women is lust and if I ever marry, I want love.'

His strong jaw line hardened. 'I can't give that to you.'

'And that's fine since I'm not going to marry you,' Rosie replied, stifling the wounded feeling that he could be so very certain that she could never inspire such finer feelings in him and then angry with herself for even thinking that way. 'Maybe you should concentrate your "trying" on trying to love our child when it's born.'

A thunderous aspect had clenched his strong features and his eyes were bright as diamonds in a dark night sky. 'You're being foolish, Rosie.'

Rosie folded her arms. 'I'm the best judge of that.'

'To turn down my offer of marriage without even properly considering it is stupid,' Alexius informed her harshly.

'We had a one-night stand, not a relationship!' Rosie slung back at him hotly, temper surging up through her like lava breaking through rocks to the surface. 'You don't know me, you don't know or care what I need or want and you walked away after that night, making it quite clear that you didn't even want to see me again!'

A very faint line of colour delineated the high arc of his exotic cheekbones. 'But I *knew* I would see you again when I took you to Greece to meet your grandfather,' he reminded her crisply.

'I don't know if I'll ever agree to that. Right now with the baby I've got enough to be getting on with in my life,' Rosie admitted, tight-mouthed.

Alexius stared at her. The luscious pink mouth that had melted beneath his had now compressed into a tough little line of obstinacy. Frustration leapt through every line of his body. He wasn't used to defiance or opposition. He wanted to bundle her up and stuff her on a plane, regardless of how she felt about it, because he *knew* that in this instance he knew best. 'Are you planning to continue cleaning every night while you're pregnant?' he asked with unconcealed scorn.

Her face burned below that derisive appraisal. 'What do you think?'

'That you need my support right now so that you can stop working…and concentrate on your exams instead,' he added reflectively, happier to picture her with books rather than a giant floor polisher almost too heavy for her to lift. 'You can hardly need to be told that the sort of work you're doing at present is too strenuous for a woman in your condition.'

Rosie had paled. 'That's nonsense. I'm managing fine—'

'You fainted,' Alexius reminded her stubbornly. 'How is that fine?'

Her fingernails bit into her palms as she clenched her hands tight on the wave of antipathy gripping her, which rose higher every time he spoke. 'Do you want to know why I fainted? I'm getting morning sickness and I can't face eating first thing so trekking over here on a nerve-racking trip to confront you was a major strain on an empty stomach. I got light-headed, that was all.'

'And if you get light-headed on a set of stairs, you will very probably fall and get injured. Am I supposed to accept that and just let you get on with it?' Alexius blasted back at her. 'What sort of man would simply accept that state of affairs without interfering?'

'The same man who had sex with me and walked out in the middle of the night without a word of explanation,' Rosie supplied without hesitation. 'Let's not pretend that you are Mr Sensitive, Mr Caring, because you're *not*.'

That condemnation still ringing in his ears, Alexius snatched up the apartment phone to communicate with his housekeeper and order breakfast for his disruptive guest. He was in a rage, a rage such as he had not felt since his teenaged years of hormonal turmoil. He was getting nowhere with her. She didn't *listen*. She had no respect. She had not even agreed to meet Socrates yet. The temper he always contained was like a wildfire seething inside him, struggling to escape the bonds of his rigid self-discipline.

'Why are you looking at me like that?' Rosie demanded unevenly, suddenly breathless at the effect of those stunning liquid mercury eyes beating down on her. 'I can look after myself, Alex. You don't need to worry about me.'

'You can look after yourself so well that you let me into your bed the first night!' Alexius hurled back at her in a lion's roar of intimidation.

Unable to argue the truth of that, Rosie didn't budge an inch or bat a single eyelash. She knew she was annoying him but suspected that anyone who said no to him annoyed him, in which case it was past time someone said no and he was forced to hear and accept it. 'Everyone makes mistakes…you were mine.'

Alexius strode forward, marvelling that she was standing her ground fearless before him when the rare sound of a raised tone issuing from his mouth sent his staff rushing for cover. How dared she call him a mistake? How dared she turn down his marriage proposal as if it were worth nothing? How dared she not listen?

'That night wasn't a mistake, *moraki mou*,' Alexius growled low in his throat, his scorching gaze locked to her triangular face, lingering on her emerald-green eyes and succulent pink mouth with an intensity that dismayed her.

Reacting to the simmering buzz of energy he put out, Rosie felt her breasts push against her sweater, her stiff, tender nipples rubbing against the scratchy wool. The hot damp sensation at her feminine core was no longer new to her, for she dreamt about that night almost every night and she was used to it now, accustomed to that nagging pulse, that ache that he had taught her to feel.

'Of course, it was a mistake,' she contradicted.

'*No*, it was not.' Alexius locked a big hand round her wrist and pulled her up against his hard muscular body. A spluttered squawk of shock erupted from Rosie before he brought his mouth crashing down on hers with a fire that burned like a naked flame on unprotected skin. He crushed her to him with a rough groan of satisfaction and kissed her with a passion that sang through her senses like a magical spell of entrapment, his tongue stabbing with erotic rhythm into the moist interior of her mouth. One minute she was knotting her hands into his luxuriant black hair to push him away and the next her fingers were delving into those silky depths in exploration and appreciation, before finally moulding to his well-shaped head to hold him close.

Alexius lowered her to the sofa and sent a hand roving up below the sweater to tease the dainty swollen peaks that had so entranced him that night three weeks earlier. Her slender spine arched, a moan of startled pleasure wrenched from her as he played with those responsive buds that were so very sensitive to his touch.

Pushing up the sweater, he bent his head to dally there with his mouth instead. A knock sounded on the door and he sprang back from her.

Returned to reality with a mortifying bang, Rosie looked down at her bare chest in horror and, wrenching her sweater back down, she sat up. 'Don't touch me like that again!'

Alexius skimmed knowing eyes like silver arrows back to her, a slumberous light in his gaze. 'Because you like it too much to say no?' he mocked as he strode to the door to open it.

Rosie's heart-shaped face was so hot it felt sunburned. He was a taker, a user. He had stolen that kiss as coolly as he had stolen her virginity and she needed more self-control around him. She certainly shouldn't be noticing that he crossed the room with the grace of a strolling tiger, all fluid rippling muscle and aggressive confidence. The real problem was that he excited her and just being in the same room with him was thrilling and there was something frighteningly seductive about the charge of that excitement. Was that excitement lust? She guessed it had to be.

Alexius settled a heavy tray down on the coffee table. 'Eat...' he urged.

There was a chocolate croissant amongst the assorted baked offerings in the bread basket and her mouth watered even as she reached for it. She poured tea and asked him politely if he wanted any, for there was a second cup.

'I only drink coffee,' he said.

She discovered that she was still trembling in the aftermath of that passionate embrace. He was *so* hot he burned her, teaching her that she was a much more physical person than she had ever imagined. It was not a discovery she was grateful to have made because it made her feel vulnerable and weak in a way she had never been before.

'Why did you get angry when I said that night was a mistake?' Rosie asked curiously.

'It was too good to be a mistake. I very much enjoyed it,' he told her with unselfconscious cool.

Rosie almost choked on her tasty mouthful of chocolate croissant and remained silent until she had swallowed it in a painful rush. 'I'll think about meeting my grandfather when my exams are over,' she conceded.

Alexius dealt her an assessing glance, noting that her belligerent streak was currently at bay. 'And will you also think then about marrying me?'

Rosie stiffened and raised her eyes as high as his slightly stubbled chin. It was a very determined, very stubborn chin with a cleft and outrageously male. 'No, that decision was clear as cut glass and I won't be revisiting it.'

Alexius released his breath in an exasperated hiss of impatience. 'Why not?'

'How can you ask me that when you don't want to get married in the first place?' Rosie prompted with raised brows signalling her astonishment at his attitude. 'Have you *ever* wanted to get married?'

'No,' he conceded.

'Have you ever wanted a child of your own?'

Alexius frowned at that unfortunate question and hesitated.

'You promised to tell me the truth from now on,' Rosie reminded him doggedly.

'No,' he admitted curtly. 'I have never wanted a child.'

'So, why on earth would I want to marry you?'

Evidently, she lacked the greed gene he was used to igniting in all her sex. 'Security? Support? A father for the child?'

'If I married you, you'd be off with another woman in five minutes flat,' Rosie forecast with a grimace at that humiliating likelihood. 'You don't strike me as the sort of guy likely to adapt easily to domesticity and parenthood either, particularly if you didn't choose either of your own free will.'

Alexius, ludicrously unused to being deemed a potential failure at anything he attempted, gritted his teeth. 'I might surprise you.'

'And pigs might fly,' Rosie remarked only half beneath her breath.

Alexius elevated a fine black brow. 'Is that a challenge?'

'No, it's not,' Rosie hastened to tell him, keen not to start another row. 'Can't we be friends, Alex?'

'I don't want to be friends with you,' Alexius shot back at her as she brushed crumbs from her lap and stood up. 'Have you eaten enough?'

'More than enough,' she insisted, glancing at her watch. 'I have a class to get to.'

Alexius lifted the phone. 'I will organise a car.'

'That's not necessary.'

'A car and driver will be at your disposal for the foreseeable future,' Alexius delivered as she walked to the door.

Rosie spun back, her eyes wide. 'Don't be ridiculous. What would I do with a car and a driver?'

'Use them,' Alexius responded without an ounce of humour. 'Give me your phone number...'

'Isn't it ironic that you're asking for it now only because I'm pregnant?' Rosie tossed at him before she could think better of it, glancing across at him to see that his handsome features clenched hard at that blunt reminder.

'We still have a lot to discuss, *moraki mou*.'

Rosie winced. 'I think I've said all I've got to say.'

A satiric smile slashed his sculpted mouth. 'While I have barely begun.'

Rosie wrote her number on a piece of paper and looked back at him. 'Don't tell my grandfather I needed time to think about meeting him, just tell him I have exams on,' she urged suddenly. 'I don't want to hurt his feelings.'

'What about mine?' Alexius quipped.

'I don't think you're over-endowed in that department,' Rosie told him frankly. 'You're too aggressive and sure of yourself to be sensitive and too selfish to be caring.'

'I just fed you,' he shot back in his own defence, disconcerted by her candour. Was that truly how she saw him?

'You're probably investing in the fact that I'm carrying the Stavroulakis heir,' she surmised, suspicion paramount as she gazed back at him, belatedly noticing the strain etched into his face and surprised by it. Did more go on beneath that smooth, sophisticated surface of his than she had supposed? Or was it the horrendous threat of the marriage he had forced himself to offer that had stressed him out? How could he do that? How could he ask her to marry him when he didn't want to get married and he didn't want a child? What had made him go against his own nature like that? Was it her grandfather's likely response to her condition and Alexius's part in it that he wished to guard against? Was that his main motivation? Marriage as a cover-up, an olive branch?

The Stavroulakis heir, not, by any stretch of imagination, a joke, Alexius mused grimly after he had instructed Titos to put a discreet bodyguard on Rosie. A child, a boy or a girl, he didn't care which. He had no preferences whatsoever. But if there was a child born, he knew that he would ensure that it enjoyed a very different childhood from the one he had endured as the last Stavroulakis heir. That was his most basic duty towards his own flesh and blood and nothing more complex.

When Rosie stuck her key in the lock the following afternoon after her classes, she was tired and still stuck firmly in a state of mental turmoil. Since the day before she had been whisked everywhere she went by a BMW and a driver, who sat around waiting for her to emerge from every class without complaint. Such a luxury felt weird in her very ordinary life, almost as weird as Alexius Stavroulakis asking her to marry him, disregarding the gulf in their social status, disregarding even the obvious fact that he neither cared for her nor wanted their baby. *Why on earth had he done that?* she asked herself in frustration. Was he crazy? She might be hugely attracted to him, but to have said yes to such a proposal would surely have been a disastrous mistake, she reflected uncertainly, her head aching from such stressful thoughts. She wanted to give her baby the best possible chance in life but was convinced that so unequal a marriage would never last.

Even worse, the fallout from a messy marital breakdown would only cause bad feeling between her and Alexius, which would in turn have an adverse effect on their child. On those grounds, it would be much wiser to build a more distant but civil relationship with Alexius outside the bonds of marriage. A relationship without intimacy or any very deep feelings, she conceded with a regret she could not stifle. But had she not so clearly seen Alexius's lack of interest or desire for either marriage or parenthood she might have been very tempted to say yes to his proposal.

Martha came downstairs, Bas cradled in her arms. 'You've got a visitor.'

Rosie walked into the lounge and stiffened in dismay when she saw Jason Steele rising from the sofa. *Oh, hell*, she thought ruefully. She was not in the mood for Jason on top of everything else she had undergone over the past forty-eight hours.

CHAPTER FIVE

'I'LL keep hold of Bas,' Martha whispered in her ear. 'He doesn't like him.'

'Thanks,' Rosie said, entering the lounge and shutting the door on the older woman. 'Well, this is a surprise, Jason. How did you find out where I lived?'

The big blond man grimaced. 'I'd sooner not say but I had to see you after what happened a couple of weeks ago,' he told her. 'All I wanted was the chance to talk to you.'

'Sit down, Jason. You scared me that night,' Rosie admitted, taking the chair opposite him.

Jason dropped back into the sofa, which creaked in protest beneath his considerable bulk. 'I'm sorry,' he told her. 'I didn't mean to do that but that guy wading in, interfering in what was none of his business, got to me. I thought you and I could go out some night… maybe see a film or go for a meal, whatever you like.'

Discomfiture at the invitation made Rosie turn pink. 'That's not a good idea—'

'Why not? What's wrong with me?' Jason asked with more than a hint of belligerence.

'I didn't say there was anything wrong with you,' Rosie hastened to assure him before deciding that in his particular case honesty probably was the best policy. 'But it wouldn't be right for either of us… I'm pregnant, Jason.'

Jason looked stunned. 'You're joking me?'

'No, I'm telling you the truth.'

'Pregnant?' he repeated, staring at her as if she'd admitted to leprosy and with something akin to disgust.

Out in the hall she heard a door opening and closing, the low timbre of male voices and Bas bursting into sudden frenzied barks.

'I didn't even know you were seeing anyone.' Jason grimaced and got back on his feet again. 'Well, this has been a waste of my time and no mistake—I don't want to date a woman expecting some other bloke's kid!'

Before Rosie could assure him that he really was quite safe from that development, the door behind her opened abruptly and all hell seemed to break loose at the same moment. Bas leapt at Jason, whom he loathed. Alexius, accompanied by the head of his security team, Titos, appeared just as Jason kicked the dog out of his path. Rosie loosed a shriek of horror as Bas flew up in the air and hit the wall before falling in a limp heap by the skirting board.

'Oh, my Lord, Jason…you've killed Bas!' she sobbed, surging forward.

'Don't upset yourself,' Alexius advised, pulling Rosie back from the dog to take her place, sliding a hand under the tiny still body, grimacing as he noted that one of Bas's legs was definitely broken, stuck out as it was at an unnatural angle. 'His heart's still beating. He's been knocked out. We'll get him straight to a vet—'

'You're a monster, Jason!' Rosie exclaimed furiously. 'First you hurt me, now you've attacked Bas—'

'The dog attacked me first!' Jason blistered back furiously. 'And I didn't mean to hurt you!'

'Everything was fine until you burst in here,' Rosie told Alexius in reproach, crouching down beside him and then flying upright again to stalk into the kitchen and snatch up a tray on which she carefully positioned the tiny dog with shaking hands.

'Call the police,' Alexius instructed Rosie. 'You have to make a complaint against Jason this time—'

'There's no need for that,' Jason began.

'There's every need,' Alexius cut in with ruthless bite. 'You followed her home from work last night... you're stalking her!'

'I'm not stalking her. I only followed you to find out where you had moved to,' Jason told Rosie ruefully. 'I didn't do you any harm. I didn't even come to the door because I knew it was too late to visit—'

Dismayed to realise that Jason had followed her home the night before, Rosie turned dazed eyes to Alexius and muttered anxiously, 'Let's get Bas to the vet first. He's the most important thing here—'

'No, *you* are,' Alexius corrected, shooting Jason a look of bitter animosity.

'I'm not going to bother her again,' Jason protested. 'I didn't even know she had a bun in the oven.'

Alexius frowned, that phrase not having come to his ears before. As he registered its meaning along with Jason's expressive shudder, Bas moaned in pain on the tray and Rosie stroked his little domed head with a tender hand while tears flooded her eyes. 'I can't bear anything to happen to Bas...he's all I've got left of Beryl!'

Alexius urged her out of the door, draping the jacket Martha passed him round her narrow shoulders. 'Beryl?' he queried, watching in consternation as tears spilled down her cheeks.

'She was my foster mum,' Rosie told him unevenly as Alexius grasped the tray and urged her into the back of the limousine waiting at the kerb. 'I moved in with her when I was twelve. It was the only place I was ever happy. She treated me like family. She really loved me—'

'Do you still see her?' Alexius prompted, keen to take her thoughts in a more positive direction for Bas was bleeding from the nose and Alexius wanted to distract her: the dog didn't look good.

Rosie dashed the tears away irritably. 'She died when I was twenty. She was ill for a long time with breast cancer. I was fifteen when it was first diagnosed and she got all the treatment but it came back the next year and the doctors couldn't do anything more…it was terminal. One of Beryl's grown-up children bought Bas as a surprise for her a few months before she died. I thought it was an insane idea to give her a pet when she was so ill, but Bas gave her an interest… He brightened those last months for her, so I couldn't let him go after she'd passed.'

The tray on her lap, she stroked the limp little animal's back with her forefinger. 'How did you know that Jason followed me home last night? How did you know he was visiting me this evening?'

'When you left yesterday I arranged for one of my security guards to keep a discreet watch on you to ensure your safety. Just as well with Jason around,' Alexius pronounced grimly.

'Why the heck would you have done that? You mean someone's been following me since yesterday?' Rosie exclaimed in disbelief.

'That's how I knew what Jason had been up to and that he had called to see you today,' Alexius pointed out tautly.

'Jason was about to leave quietly when you let in Bas and everything went pear-shaped. I don't need a security guard,' she said thinly. 'What am I? A princess or something? I've got nothing worth stealing. Where are we going?'

'A veterinary clinic where Bas will get immediate treatment.'

Rosie stared down at the chihuahua's still little body, noticed the blood at his nose and her lower lip quivered. 'I love him so much it's ridiculous. He's not very well trained and Jason teased him so much when I lived with Mel that he hates men.'

'He bit me as well,' Alexius volunteered.

'At least you didn't kick him,' Rosie muttered.

Alexius surveyed Bas and suppressed a sigh, wondering if that was all he had in his favour. Saving Bas to bite another day was clearly a priority when the mother of his child was so deeply attached to him. His own mother had had several pet dogs and had appeared fond of them, a great deal fonder than she had ever been of her son. He studied Rosie as she sat next to him, slim as a willow wand and without an ounce of surplus weight. He wondered if it was healthy for a pregnant woman to be so thin, tried to picture that tiny body swollen with his child and was startled by the sudden flush of heat that gave him an instant erection. How could that image be a turn-on? he asked himself in disbelief. Any fool could get a woman pregnant, he reasoned. There was nothing remotely special about it, although the process that brought it about had been pure bliss, he recalled in a helpless surge of sensual recall as the limo reached their destination.

Alexius removed the tray from Rosie and carried Bas into the animal clinic. A veterinary nurse in an overall came forward to collect him and then a burly vet emerged to greet them and ask questions.

'We need to X-ray him and stabilise him first. He's got concussion and the leg needs to be treated. If we're lucky, it may not be more serious than that.'

As the vet spoke Bas suffered a seizure that sent convulsions travelling through his little body and made his three working legs paddle in the air. Rosie gasped in alarm and tried to soothe him.

'I'm afraid that's not a good sign but there's nothing you can do to stop it,' the vet warned her before he directed them to the waiting room and took Bas into the surgery to check him out.

'This is one of the most highly acclaimed private animal clinics in the UK,' Alexius assured Rosie. 'If Bas can be saved, it'll happen here.'

Rosie stared into space, trying to imagine life without Bas's lively loving presence and shrinking from it. Thirty minutes later, the nurse appeared and told them that Bas would have to spend the night under observation because he might yet require emergency surgery on his fractured skull.

'How on earth am I going to pay the bills for all this?' Rosie whispered in dismay as Alexius vaulted upright, clearly grateful to be freed to leave. 'This level of emergency treatment and care must cost a fortune.'

'I'm taking care of it,' Alexius fielded, reaching down a hand to draw her out of her chair. She was light as feather and so preoccupied by her pet's plight and prospects that she was wholly divorced from his presence. Being ignored was, he discovered, a novel experience he didn't much appreciate, particularly when the woman doing the ignoring was dressed in worn jeans, tacky trainers and an overlarge tee with a garish logo on the front. Somehow her complete indifference to her appearance around him added to his growing sense of affront. He gazed down at her, noticing the way the artificial light burnished her hair to silvery fairness...and her nipples caused little dents in the tee. He tensed, remembering the tormentingly sweet taste of those little buds and her wild responsiveness and had to struggle to get his mind back on the conversation.

'That's very generous of you but I don't like being under an obligation,' Rosie admitted, almost stumbling on the steps outside the clinic until Alexius grabbed her arm to steady her.

'Agree to meet your grandfather and I'll write the debt off,' Alexius responded, stunning silver eyes framed by lush black lashes and strikingly noticeable in his lean bronzed face.

Rosie was sharply disconcerted by the suggestion and stared up at him in disbelief. 'But that's blackmail.'

'That's me, *moraki mou*,' Alexius returned without apology. 'I'm programmed to make the most of any advantage and if I can do your grandfather a good turn in the process, I will do it.'

Rosie breathed in deep and slow, shaken that he could be quite so unashamed of his ruthless and immoral approach to life. So, his generosity had a price? Was she really surprised by the fact? Alexius Stavroulakis wasn't the kind of guy to do something for nothing. But the source of her concern was very real, for she was convinced that the bill for treating Bas would run into thousands of pounds and there was no way that she could pay any of it back. 'Neither a borrower nor a lender be,' Beryl used to say in warning, and Rosie had always respected that maxim because on a small income if she did not live within her means she risked getting into serious trouble. But how much of a sacrifice would she really be making if she agreed to go to Greece? In the back of her mind she was already coming round to accepting that curiosity alone would have prompted her to meet her grandfather. But in truth, and it was very much a visceral reaction, she did *want* to meet her father's father and find out more about the Greek side of her family.

'I sit my last exam on the fifteenth,' Rosie conceded tautly. 'I'll be free to travel to Greece for a visit after that.'

'You see, I'm easy to deal with,' Alexius murmured smoothly, relieved that he had something positive to tell his godfather that would lighten the tiresome restrictions of his convalescence. The news that Rosie was pregnant would be a good deal less welcome to a man of Socrates's generation and traditional outlook but nothing could be done about that, Alexius reasoned wryly.

'No, you're not. You're devious and cold-blooded and you're using my affection for Bas as a weapon against me,' Rosie censured curtly, treating him to a look of condemnation. 'Don't expect me to like you for that.'

'I saved the dog's life by bringing him here,' Alexius countered levelly. 'I have one further request to make…'

'Go on,' Rosie encouraged, climbing into the limousine and this time taking account of the opulent leather and fittings with wide, wondering eyes. Was this how he usually travelled? Nothing could have more accurately delineated the gulf between them, she thought uncomfortably.

'I'd like you to see Dmitri Vakros and have your pregnancy officially confirmed. I also want to be sure that you're in good health.'

'I've already seen a doctor and been checked over,' Rosie protested wearily.

'Do you instinctively argue against everything I suggest?' Alexius shot back at her in exasperation, marvelling at the amount of feisty distrust and obstinacy etched into her face. She might be tiny but she had the heart of a lion. 'I'm thinking of your well-being.'

Rosie dragged her eyes from his, her attention straying accidentally to the long powerful thigh so close to her own and up to the fabric cupping the sizeable bulge of his crotch, her colour heightening as she hurriedly lifted her head again. Images of him in bed with her, that lean bronzed body entwined erotically with her own, filled her head in Technicolor and for an instant her mouth ran dry and she could hardly breathe for excitement. Not embarrassment, *excitement*, she scolded herself furiously, wondering what he had done to her thinking processes. 'My well-being is really none of your business.'

'If it's my baby, it's my business,' Alexius contradicted in a roughened undertone.

Rosie bit her soft lower lip to strangle an acid response before it leapt off her tongue. He wasn't interested in their baby and she knew he wasn't, so he could only be going through the motions of what he felt was expected from him. But would it be wise to discourage even the most minor display of interest on his part? She might not want a reluctant husband, but if it was possible she did want a father for her baby and including him in the process was an inescapable part of that, no matter how much the necessity warred against her private feelings. He had walked away from her after a one-night stand but she had to learn to live with that, take it on the chin, move on from that humiliation to concentrate on more important things.

'Rosie…' Alexius growled. 'Will you agree to see Dmitri?'

'If I must,' Rosie sighed.

'Surely you can see that I must take responsibility for you now?'

Green eyes glinting, Rosie lifted her chin. 'It's been years since I needed anyone to take responsibility for me. I'm not a child. I'm an adult. I can look after myself.'

'You'll have to get used to me doing it from now on,' Alexius imparted with stinging cool.

Her teeth gritted. 'I'm afraid not. I'm very independent. If I wanted to lean on you I'd have agreed to marry you,' she pointed out waspishly.

Alexius was gritting his teeth as well, the reminder of her rejection unwelcome. 'You may still change your mind—'

'I don't think so. You're not the kind of guy I want to marry,' Rosie told him ruefully.

Eyes glittering with high voltage annoyance, Alexius breathed in deep, wondering why he wasn't more relieved by her assurance, by the freedom left untouched by her decision. He didn't want to get married, he had *never* wanted to get married any more than he had ever wanted a child. Nothing had changed but even as he thought that his attention swerved back to the small figure in the far corner of his limo. Her pale frosted hair shone in the street lights filtering through the windows, accentuating her delicate profile, and renewed desire burned through him like a torch. She was a part of his life now but not a part he had spontaneously chosen and it infuriated him that he should still want her even in such challenging circumstances. He needed a woman in his bed, he needed a woman badly, he told himself grimly. There was no other explanation for his illogical response to her.

'What sort of a guy do you want to marry?' Alexius enquired very drily.

Rosie went pink. 'Someone kind, honest and straightforward.'

Well aware that in her eyes he failed in every one of those categories, his ego dented, Alexius compressed his handsome mouth and made copious excuses for himself. Socrates had put him in the position of not being honest or straightforward when they first met. He had intended to be kind when it came to the dog but, when he had realised he could use the cost of the treatment as a lever to influence events, his more devious ruthless side had surged to the fore. So, he wasn't perfect, not Mr Sensitive or Mr Caring as she had put it, he recalled grimly. A woman had never criticised him before and she had already done it more than once. *Thee mou* and he had asked her to *marry* him? He must have been out of his mind, thinking of long, hot nights in her bed rather than meeting with a constant litany of complaints and critical comments.

Rosie watched Alexius from below her lashes, wondering at the simmering tension revealed by the hard set of his cheekbones and the cast of his strong jaw. He was definitely not in a good mood. But he ought to be grateful that she had turned down his marriage proposal and prevented him from offering himself up as an old-fashioned sacrifice to convention. Some day he would meet a woman whom he really did want to marry. She stiffened at that idea, discovered in astonishment that she was outrageously possessive of the father of her child and didn't at all relish the concept of him taking up with another woman. That was downright unreasonable, she told herself sternly. The night before she had put his name in a search engine and found a whole cache of images that proved that Alexius Kolovos Stavroulakis was a womaniser of many years' standing. He had been bedding glamorous models, socialites and stars since he was a teenager and he always moved on quickly again to fresh fields. Seemingly he had never had a single long-lasting relationship with a woman, had not even lived with one, and that told Rosie that she had made the right decision. He was shockingly wealthy and even more shockingly successful in the business world, an unemotional and famously shrewd tycoon, whom few people professed to know well. There was no way she could ever be happy with a guy like that. They were ill suited in every possible way on a level that went beyond wealth, status and education. She could not even begin to imagine the life he had led.

'I'll be in touch,' Alexius murmured flatly as she got out of the limo. 'Good luck with your exams!'

Rosie turned her head back in surprise and grinned, her smile lighting up her eyes and illuminating her face to quite exquisite effect. Alexius studied her stonily, refusing to admire or appreciate, his every response locked down. 'Thanks,' she said breezily.

Martha was waiting to hear about Bas and Rosie brought her up to date, telling her that she would call to ask how the little dog was the next morning. 'They said they'd phone if anything happened before that,' she said.

She made supper and could hardly stop yawning. Her GP had warned her that pregnancy would make her feel more tired than usual. Resolving to be up early to study the next day, she fell into bed, involuntarily recalled the night with Alexius and lay in the darkness, feeling the feverish heat in her pelvis tug at her with dissatisfaction. He had taught her to want sex, she decided in disgust. In time she would get over that longing and over him as well. For now she was just a little bit obsessed with him, she acknowledged uneasily.

CHAPTER SIX

'IT'S A blob,' Alexius pronounced, frowning at the sonograph machine, striving and failing to see and feel the same response that had made Rosie's big green eyes well up with sentimental tears.

'It's a baby,' his friend Dmitri contradicted while the nurse wiped the gel from Rosie's still-flat stomach. 'Your son or daughter.'

'Alex hasn't got that much imagination,' Rosie commented, sliding down off the examination couch with relief. She hadn't wanted Alexius present during the scan and had agreed purely on the strength of the conviction that if he was to feel that this was *his* baby she had to involve him in her pregnancy whenever it was possible. So much for that. *It's a blob!* she reflected in despair.

'Well, there's nothing much to see yet,' Alexius countered defensively, wishing he hadn't bothered to ask to be present, wishing he had just stayed out of the whole damned debate. He was at a total loss when people got slushy and emotional. That had never been his thing.

They adjourned to Dmitri's office where his friend pointed out that the blob looked big for a woman of Rosie's small proportions and that a Caesarean delivery might be necessary. Instantly, Alexius felt queasy and guilty as hell as in his mind the blob became a serious threat to Rosie's survival. Suppose she died, he thought suddenly, the shock of the concept whipping up a melodramatic storm of deathbed scenes inside his mind that proved he had far more imagination than Rosie would ever suspect. He studied her, engaged as she was in animated chatter with the obstetrician he had first met as a medical student at university. Delicate colour warmed her small face, enthusiasm lifted her usually quiet voice and sparkled in her eyes. She wanted the blob, she really, *really* wanted the blob, he registered in amazement. Pregnancy might have messed up her life and her plans but even so she was prepared to go with the flow and make room for his baby now. As a male whose parents had never made room for him in their lives, he was deeply impressed by her unselfishness and willingness to adapt to the new order.

'Didn't you feel *anything*…even when you heard its heartbeat?' Rosie pressed hopefully, moving back to the limo at the kerb. 'I found that really exciting!'

Shrewd gaze screened, Alexius glanced at Rosie. The most exciting part of his day had happened when she emerged from her home, clad in a short black stretchy skirt and a fitted top that outlined her sleek little body to perfection. He was still enjoying the view of her long shapely legs, well, they were long in proportion to the rest of her, he reasoned, and that sweet little swell of her bottom when she bent over right in front of him to fix her shoe was downright indecent. He only had to think of sinking into the hot, wet, velvet welcome of her and he was hard as a rock and feverishly hungry to enjoy what he had enjoyed only once before. And that wasn't like him. In fact, more and more he was feeling uneasy inside his own skin around Rosie. He should be moving on to pastures new. Rosie was already the past and, even though she would essentially be part of his future as well once she had the blob, he should be delighted that she wasn't trying to nail him down to fully committed partner and parenting duties and promises of everlasting fidelity: he was still free as a bird, he reminded himself doggedly, disappointed when no spark of anticipation ignited at the prospect of his next lover. Of course, he was thirty-one years old and he had had an active sex life from around the age of sixteen when one of his mother's friends had seduced him. When it came to women, he had had more freedom, experience and choice than most men enjoyed and it was possible that he was currently a little jaded.

Rosie was deeply disappointed by Alexius's lack of a warm response to the sonogram picture of their future son or daughter. She wondered why he had bothered to come and she had noticed how squeamish he had been when Dmitri Vakros mentioned the possibility of a Caesarean. Alexius had turned a grey shade, his look of horror unhidden. He was such a *bloke*. She already had an emotional connection with the child she carried but possibly she was expecting too much too soon from a guy who had only known for a week that fatherhood was on his horizon. Did it loom like a black cloud, she wondered, or as something new and different?

Alexius breathed in deep. 'I'm taking you to get measured for a new wardrobe.'

Rosie settled disbelieving eyes on him. 'You're… *what*?'

'You need to dress up for Greece and you haven't

got the clothes for it. I don't want you to feel uncomfortable in your grandfather's home,' Alexius admitted.

Rosie was enraged at his confident assumption that he knew how she would feel about anything. 'I don't care about stuff like that!'

'You think you don't but you will,' Alexius forecast, reckoning that she was planning to be as stubborn about the clothes as she was about everything else. Everything was a battle with Rosie: she hated him calling the shots but all his life he'd been a dominant personality and he had no plans to change.

'And how the heck do you make that out? Is my grandfather as wealthy as you are?' she suddenly demanded.

'No, but he is a multimillionaire,' Alexius revealed for the first time. 'And he and his family enjoy a comfortable lifestyle.'

'A multimillionaire?' Rosie gasped in panic. 'Truthfully?'

'Truthfully,' Alexius confirmed.

Rosie was silenced, irritated that she had not suspected that reality for herself. After all, how likely was it that someone as rich as Alexius would have a godfather who was an ordinary man on a middling income? Suddenly she felt intimidated by what might await her in Greece.

'I don't want you to look and feel like a poor relation when you meet your father's family,' Alexius admitted.

'Even if it's the truth?' she fielded between gritted teeth. 'Why should I care about what I look like? That's superficial.'

'I agree but that's how the world is,' he responded with irrefutable logic. 'Appearances are important.'

Her thin shoulders hunched. 'I don't want you spending any more money on me, and I can't afford a new wardrobe,' she pointed out flatly.

'The cost is nothing to me,' Alexius retorted with a grimace.

'But not when it came to fixing up Bas?' she queried sharply, thinking with relief of how well the little dog had recovered while studying Alexius, wishing he were not so beautiful that he kept on ensnaring her attention. No matter how desperately hard she tried not to look at him her gaze repeatedly swerved back to him. Her entire body tingled as she remembered the raw sensuality of his mouth on hers and the air in her lungs shortened as if she were zooming down too fast on a roller-coaster ride.

'I would have covered the dog's needs no matter what you did,' Alexius countered levelly, his libido reacting to the buzz of sexual energy in the atmosphere so that he had to fight the urge to simply grab her. All those years of sexual practice and sophistication, he thought grimly, and all he wanted to do was flatten her to the seat like a marauder and have her any way she would let him. For the first time ever with a woman he was being cautious.

'But I didn't know that!' Rosie yelled back at him furiously in one of the sudden explosions of temper that always took him by surprise. 'How was I supposed to know that?'

'I'm not a monster… You're carrying my baby—'

'You mean, the blob?' Rosie snapped nastily.

Slight colour tinged his exotic cheekbones and his handsome mouth folded. 'It *did* look like a blob. Was

I supposed to lie to the woman who told me she valued honesty?'

Out of nowhere a surge of stinging tears assailed
Rosie's eyes and she blinked them back hurriedly and
reached spontaneously for the hand braced on the space
between them. 'No, I don't want you to feel that you
have to lie or pretend for my sake… I don't *ever* want
you to feel like th-that!' she stammered.

'You're crying!' Alexius noticed, aghast at the development.

'No, it's OK…OK!' Rosie exclaimed, frantically
grabbing at and stroking his hand in apology. 'Remember what Dmitri said? My hormones are all over
the place at the moment… The tears just come for no
good reason—'

'That doesn't make sense,' Alexius pronounced, logical to the nth degree and hooking his hand into hers to
draw her onto his lap without even thinking about it.
Getting his arms round her tiny body at last felt amazingly good. 'I'm sorry I called the baby a blob and hurt
your feelings.'

Rosie twisted to look at him with big, round green
eyes. 'Are you feeling all right?'

In surely the most awkward position ever allot-
ted to a man on the make, Alexius caught her chin
and claimed the delicious moistness of her mouth and
kissed her with devouring urgency. Rosie shivered in
eager response, feeling her body light up on all sys-
tems go inside her skin. As she twisted, Alexius lifted
her and brought her round sideways, pushing her bottom into stirring contact with his healthy erection. Her
eyes opened even wider as a deft hand travelled up her

skirt and slid between her thighs to cup the heart of her where she ached. 'Alex!' she gasped.

He wrenched up the skirt and fought with her panties to access the warm, welcoming wetness of his fantasies, and he groaned with satisfaction against her swollen mouth as he got there and discovered that she was as ready as he was. His thumb circled her clitoris and set off a chain reaction through her pelvis that she could not control. She writhed, she moaned, made not the smallest attempt to escape, intoxicated as she was by the way he was teasing her overexcited body. She buried her mouth against his strong brown throat, kissing him, drinking in the glorious hot male scent of his flesh like an addict, all of her senses up and away on a magical tour of reacquaintance. With one finger, he slid inside and she ground down her bottom onto the thrust of his arousal, helpless in the grip of the most driving need she had ever experienced, feeling the gathering storm at the heart of her, rising up through her like an unstoppable force of nature. She splintered from the inside out with the intensity of the pleasure, her body jerking in the successive spasms of ecstasy, her head falling weakly against his shoulder in the aftermath.

'Feel better, *latria mou*?' Alexius prompted thickly, wanting so much more but satisfied to have smashed the platonic barriers she had set up between them.

'Like I've died and gone to heaven,' she whispered honestly, daring to open her eyes, catch a glimpse of the busy city street the limo was traversing and shocked by the sight. 'I can't believe you just did what you did.'

Alexius released his pent-up breath slowly above her head and held on tight to her with both arms, sealing them both into the intimacy she had sought to deny.

He had been tempted to whip off that last barrier and sink deep into her but in fact he could hardly believe he had gone as far as he had in the back of a limo either. It wasn't him—he was a conventional guy. He didn't *do* stuff like this. There was something about her that made him more spontaneous, not that he thought that was much of an excuse for behaving like a horny teenager. She lifted her tousled head and gave him a guilty but sunny smile of appreciation. It made him feel ten feet tall and the painful throb of his own unsated body receded in receipt of it.

'Oh, my goodness,' Rosie mumbled, lifting her arms to break his hold and scramble off him again. 'I'm sorry, I'm so selfish... I didn't do anything for you—'

'It's not a problem,' Alexius drawled.

But Rosie could see from the cut of his trousers that there was a problem, a very big problem from his point of view. It was, however, a decidedly positive revelation for Rosie to realise that he could still summon up that amount of desire for a body she had always regarded as not that desirable on male terms. 'You know I *could*... I mean, I haven't done *that* before but I'm sure you could give me directions—'

In receipt of that offer, Alexius was startled when he found himself laughing out loud and he gave her a heart-stopping smile that welded her embarrassed eyes to him. 'Not in the back of a car in broad daylight. Some other time... I'll survive. Touching you again was worth it,' he told her huskily.

Hot colour washed Rosie's face and she suddenly felt incredibly shy and unsure of herself.

'Come home with me after we do the wardrobe thing,' Alexius urged.

It was the key for confusion and indecision to engulf Rosie like a tidal wave because she suffered instantaneous cold feet. 'Wouldn't it be wiser to write off what just happened as a little slip?'

The last glimmerings of his smile died away. He stared steadily back at her, his gorgeous eyes pained. 'A mistake *and* a little slip? Is that the sum total of what we have?'

'You're the best judge of that,' Rosie whispered, knowing she was already in so deep with him she might as well have been buried alive. The raw sexual attraction between them was undeniable but were there any other layers for him beyond her conception of the blob?

On her side of the fence, layer was piling onto layer with regard to her feelings about Alexius Stavroulakis. She couldn't look at him—even when he was being difficult—without wanting him. She couldn't look at him without thinking that he was beautiful. He was absolutely never out of her thoughts. He had insisted on accompanying her to pick up Bas when he was released from the animal clinic and had turned up with a plush new basket for her pet. He also unfailingly phoned her every day to check that she was all right, although he never seemed to have much to say when he did call and the silences gnawed on her nerves until she learned to fill those awkward moments with inconsequential chatter. She was falling in love with Alexius and had no idea how to call a halt to that seemingly inevitable process, even though she knew that she was only storing up trouble for the future.

A svelte stylist took Rosie's measurements and questioned her about her clothing preferences. Rosie made no objection and she was very much ashamed of her change of heart. But after what had happened in the limousine with Alexius she was ridiculously reluctant to argue with him again. She had noticed that he had told her very little about her grandfather and his family yet clearly he knew them all. She was convinced that if Alexius was advising her to dress up there was probably a good reason for it and she cringed at the suspicion that her grandfather might well be embarrassed by a cheaply and casually clad granddaughter who clearly came from a much poorer background. Could she come to care for people who were willing to judge her purely on her appearance?

The limo drew up outside the building where she lived and Alexius gave her a look, an ebony brow slanting up in wicked question, and she knew exactly what he was silently asking, wished she didn't, wished even more that her treacherous body didn't leap at the prospect of going to bed with him again. It would just be sex, no doubt fantastic sex, but it would only complicate things. It was, she acknowledged, a great shame that she had slept with Alexius before she got to know him, but what was done was done and if they did become intimate again she wanted her brain rather than her body to make that decision for her.

One last exam and then Greece, she told herself encouragingly. Her mind would be clearer then, her instincts less prone to her present horrendous desire to lean on Alexius for support. That wasn't a good idea because he might not be there for the long haul…only time would tell. But what if he was already prepared to phone some other woman to satisfy the need she had stirred up? That fear kept Rosie awake half the night as she finally accepted that she couldn't have it both ways, no matter how much she wanted to. Either *she* slept with Alexius or accepted that he would eventually and maybe even sooner sleep with someone else.

CHAPTER SEVEN

ROSIE sat on the wonderfully comfortable seat, buckled up for take-off. The seat was comfy but she was not. The sheer opulence of the private jet spooked her. Bas lay in his basket on the seat beside her, slumped in an awkward pose, one front leg enclosed in a cast. He was quieter since the assault, more nervous too, Rosie conceded with regret, frantic to think of anything other than the forthcoming ordeal of meeting her father's family in Athens. She didn't feel like herself any more, not sheathed in the very elegant little green dress that nipped in at her bust, waist and hips to give her a shape she had not known she had. Every garment had been professionally altered to suit her height and she didn't even want to think about how much money such perfect tailoring might have cost. Used to shopping in children's departments to find any kind of a fit, Rosie was unnerved by the fashionable expensive clothing that had been delivered to her bedsit to fill not only one but three accompanying suitcases. Would she be expected to change clothes several times a day like a member of the royal family?

Her exams were over but she had not been free to go out on the town with her classmates to celebrate the night before. Not only could she not drink but she had also been reluctant to face Alexius with bruised eyes and the pallor of someone who had stayed out too late. But since when had she become so concerned about what she looked like? That new pitiful self-consciousness that had her sitting in high heels that flattered her legs but that nonetheless pinched like the very devil infuriated Rosie. Everything that had once mattered to her from her fierce independence to her freedom seemed to have been wrenched from her. She thought of her baby and mentally apologised to it for her troubled mood.

Meanwhile, gloriously unaware of the doubts and insecurities assailing his passenger, indeed assuming that she was looking forward to meeting her wealthy relatives, Alexius worked with determination at his laptop on the other side of the saloon. Watching her board, her pale hair bouncing on her shoulders and shining in the sunlight, her chin lifting in challenge when she saw his attention lingering, had been quite sufficient. He saw her, he *wanted* her like a starving man faced with a banquet: it was that simple, that shamefully basic. And Alexius didn't like feeling like that one little bit. Subjected to that galling heat when he least welcomed it, he brooded on the mystery of it and longed to shake free of it. The maddening hunger she had infected him with like a virus outraged his pride and threatened his self-control. He wondered if greater access to that enticing little body would provide the cure that would kill the constant ache of arousal and programme his brain back to cold normality. He would get bored with her— he always got bored with his lovers, he reflected with sudden satisfaction.

'Where will I be staying tonight?' Rosie asked abruptly.

'At your grandfather's…' Alexius raised a questioning black brow at the expression of dismay his answer had earned. 'What's the problem?'

'I assumed I'd be staying at a hotel… I mean, I don't know these people and it's not going to help that I arrive pregnant and unmarried, is it?' Rosie pointed out apprehensively. 'It could be very uncomfortable for me.'

'That's an understandable concern,' Alexius positively purred, delighted to step into the breach in her hour of apparent need. 'I should have thought of that. You'll want to get to know Socrates at a more relaxed pace than you would enjoy as a house guest.'

'Yes…' Rosie awarded him a look of relief at his grasp of her plight. 'I'm glad you can see that.'

'I'm not as insensitive as you like to believe,' Alexius told her, a shot of adrenalin firing through him, his devious streak having a field day at her expense. On a high of gratification, he stood up and even bent down to stroke a daring forefinger over Bas's exposed spine as he moved past. Bas twisted his head round, his bat ears unfurling like sails, and bared his crooked teeth in a growled warning that Alexius should keep his distance.

'*No*, Bas,' Rosie said firmly.

Suppressing a revealing grin, Alexius buzzed the steward to pour drinks. Suddenly he felt like punching the air: this was his chance to take her home with him!

A couple of hours later, Rosie sat rigid in the limo whisking them out to the suburbs where Socrates Seferis lived, her nervous tension pronounced. 'Who else lives with my grandfather?'

'Currently only your aunt Sofia.'

Rosie's spine eased down a little. 'Do we admit that I'm pregnant… I mean, how are we going to broach *that*?' she pressed with a wince of discomfort at the prospect. She didn't even know these people but right from the start she would feel at a disadvantage.

'We're not dependent teenagers, Rosie.'

'The way we behaved we might as well have been.'

'I will deal with it. You don't need to say anything.'

'Maybe you should just let it go for the moment—it's not like I'm showing yet.'

His beautiful, wilful mouth tightened. 'On this issue, I prefer honesty from the outset.'

She resisted the temptation to say that she wished that had always been his attitude. The limo purred up a driveway to a large impressive modern house set in manicured gardens. She climbed out, gripping Alexius's hand to steady herself when she teetered on her heels.

'You can hardly walk in those shoes,' Alexius censured.

'But they look good,' she countered flatly. 'And according to you that's all that matters.'

'It wouldn't matter to me if you walked barefoot.'

Considering that he had not been put off by her cleaning uniform, she gave considerable weight to that remark. A manservant received them in a large airy hall and then a heavily built older man with grizzled grey hair strode out of one of the rooms to survey her with keen eyes and a wide welcoming smile. 'Rosie?'

The warmth of his greeting dispelled her worst tension and she gave him a shy smile. 'Grandad…?'

'And Alexius.' The man by her side was welcomed with an open affection that seemed to make her companion's lean darkly handsome features set in even

tauter lines. For the first time, it occurred to Rosie that
Alexius, for whatever reasons—and she didn't want to
think about that—had not been looking forward to this
meeting in the slightest. 'Smile,' Socrates urged. 'This
is a day of celebration. You've brought my grandchild
home to me.'

They were ushered into a large sunlit room and a
small blonde woman, who looked to be in her forties
and had sharp, not unattractive features moved forward
to introduce herself as Sofia. Her smile didn't reach her
eyes. Her father began to ask Rosie a stream of eager
questions, his interest in her likes, dislikes and hobbies
rather touching for a young woman who had never before found herself the focus of so much attention. The
older man's grasp of English was not the equal of his
godson's, however, and several times Alexius stepped
in like an interpreter to clarify her answers. When she
told Socrates about her studies, he beamed at her in approval, and she would have mentioned her plans to go to
university had she not been thinking that with a baby in
tow that might yet prove an impossible challenge. The
more Socrates talked to Rosie, the more stiff and silent
Sofia became until eventually she closed a determined
hand to Rosie's forearm. 'You and I need to get better
acquainted. I've got photos of the family to show you,'
she said, urging Rosie across the room to a sofa and
settling a large album down on her lap.

'I can't help being really curious about this family,'
Rosie admitted, leafing through the album while Sofia
put a label to innumerable faces. She recognised her
own father as a teenager in a beach photograph, good-
looking, smiling and surrounded by girls. It was a fair
match for the faded photo that was all her mother had

had to show for her affair with Troy Seferis. When Rosie's aunt pointed out her uncle, Timon, Rosie asked if she would be meeting him as well.

Sofia frowned. 'I don't know. Timon is in rehab again. I'm afraid my brother has been a drug addict since he was seventeen and my father is still struggling without success to straighten him out.'

Rosie absorbed that sad news without comment, wishing that Alexius had forewarned her and desperately searching for a safer topic of conversation. 'Can you tell me anything about my father, Troy?' she prompted hopefully.

'Only that with the exception of my father the men in this family are and were fairly useless,' Sofia told her in a tart undertone. 'Timon has two sons but while they were working in one of Dad's hotels they set up a scam to skim off money for themselves.'

Rosie was taken aback at that admission of her cousins' criminality. 'My goodness...' she remarked uncertainly just as her grandfather sprang up out of his chair on the other side of the room with surprising vigour and spat something in guttural Greek at Alexius, which sent her startled eyes flying in that direction instead. 'What's happened?'

Alexius's body was rigid and unyielding, his face hard and expressionless. Rosie had never seen his innate reserve so pronounced. His godfather was ranting at him and Alexius was saying very little in response.

'*Thee mou*, you might look ladylike and quiet but you're clearly a very clever little schemer,' Sofia commented, shooting Rosie a look of tremendous satisfaction.

Realising that her aunt understood the source of the

conflict between the two men and very much afraid that she did as well, Rosie composed her face and said, 'And why would you think that?'

'Falling pregnant by a billionaire is a world-class coup and surely no accident on your part? Not with a mother who pulled the same stunt on my younger brother!' Sofia jibed with a chuckle of unconcealed amusement and derision. 'And to think I thought you were coming here to charm and impress my father. Instead, he's shocked and furious…'

Allowing her aunt's cheap, unfeeling sneer to roll off her, Rosie pressed urgently, 'What's your father saying to Alexius?'

'This is as good as a soap opera,' the older woman commented with enjoyment. 'According to my anti-quated father, your reputation is now ruined for all time…'

Well, we'll see about that, Rosie reflected in exasperation, rising from her seat in a quick movement and advancing to within a few feet of the two angry men. Alexius might not be shouting but she knew by his powerful stance and the wild, stormy glitter of his eyes that he was furious and that only his respect for the older man was making him withstand the tirade in silence.

'Stay out of this,' Alexius breathed tautly, when he realised Rosie was at his elbow.

'No, it's not fair and it's not the Dark Ages either!' Rosie protested, fixing her attention on her red-faced grandfather and addressing him directly. '*Please* calm down. I wouldn't have come if I'd known I was likely to cause so much trouble between you and Alexius. It can't be good for your heart to get so worked up…and don't say anything more to Alexius. He did ask me to marry him.'

'You...*did*?' Socrates turned back to stare at his god-son in astonishment, his anger visibly falling away at that information.

'And I said no,' Rosie slotted in before her grand-father could get too excited about what was not going to happen.

'*No?*' her grandfather thundered back at her instead. 'Are you insane? You're carrying his child and you said *no*?'

'I think we should let the dust settle on this and leave for now,' Rosie suggested tightly, laying a trembling hand on Alexius's sleeve. 'I can come back to visit when tempers cool...if I'm still welcome, of course.'

'Of course, you will be,' Alexius pronounced with unbelievable cool as if nothing whatsoever had happened. 'It is I who will not be so.'

'If you're not marrying him, you shouldn't be going anywhere with him,' Socrates Seferis delivered in a final cutting piece of advice.

Rosie glanced from her grandfather's angry, dissatisfied face to her aunt's barely hidden triumph at Rosie's fast fall from grace and decided that she had had enough of the family reunion for one day. 'I make my own decisions and I trust Alexius,' she said quietly.

'Why on earth didn't you stand up for yourself?' Rosie demanded of Alexius once they were back in the car. 'He's the one who told you to get to know me.'

'I have great respect for Socrates, *moli mou*. He said nothing that was not deserved. I *do* have the reputation of a womaniser and I should, for once, have practised restraint.' Yet even in the midst of that, Alexius was hopelessly amused and oddly touched by the manner in which Rosie had waded in like a miniature prize fighter to try and defend him to her grandfather, failing to appreciate that Socrates was probably the only man alive whom Alexius would have allowed to speak to him in such terms.

'Maybe *I* should have kept my hands off *you*,' Rosie muttered, irritated that he was trying to shoulder all the blame as if she were some helpless little fluttery thing with no brains between her ears.

'No, I wanted you and I am too used to taking what I want and not counting the cost,' Alexius breathed with a raw edge. 'That, at least, was a fair comment.'

'You should've listened to me when I told you not to mention me being pregnant so soon.' Rosie sighed, wishing he were not so highly resistant to accepting advice.

'The least I owed my godfather was the truth.'

'My aunt is poisonous—she really enjoyed that awful scene. Why didn't you warn me what she was like?'

'I didn't want to influence your opinions before you met them. They're not my family, after all,' he traded. 'As a rule, Socrates is a liberal, warm-hearted man but he has your quick temper. He will very much regret the way you parted. I underestimated his reaction. His values are naturally those of the older generation and I should have foreseen that.'

Alexius took her back to the airport and it was a shock when they were suddenly engulfed in a seething mass of people waving cameras and shouting questions. She shrank into Alexius's side, blinded by the flash bulbs going off all around her, barely aware of the security men struggling to keep the crush at bay.

'Who's the girl?' voices shouted repeatedly. 'What about Adrianna Lesley?'

Journalists, Rosie labelled belatedly, what she supposed were called paparazzi, she guessed as, his handsome mouth clenched, Alexius herded her silently through the building where everybody was staring, no doubt wondering who they were. Although as the airport security staff joined in with Alexius's own team to practise crowd control in keeping the most overenthusiastic members of the press from preventing their free passage, she began to appreciate that Alexius appeared to be exceedingly well-known and that ironically it was her presence in his company that was creating the stir. At the back of her mind, she was trying very hard not to wonder who Adrianna was. A girlfriend? What did she know about his private life?

'Sorry about that,' Alexius pronounced, reading the shock at the onslaught of the paps in her dazed expression after he had slotted her into a helicopter and Bas arrived in his pet carrier.

'How often does that happen to you?' Rosie whispered shakily, shooting a troubled glance his way.

'Too often.'

'Why were they so curious about me?'

'You arrived in my private jet. I'm rarely seen travelling with a woman. Someone at the airport probably tipped them off.' His voice was clipped, offhand, as if such incidents were so common in his daily life that he didn't even think about them. But what his tone seemed to say was misleading because for the first time ever Alexius had been enraged by a press intrusion. Rosie had been frightened and she was pregnant and it shouldn't have happened. He had felt like scooping her up into his arms to shield her but had known such behaviour would only serve to incite the paparazzi to even greater aggression.

'Where are we going now?' she asked on the back of a huge yawn as she idly stroked Bas's ear through the bars of his carrier.

'Somewhere private,' Alexius breathed, flexing his big shoulders below his finely tailored jacket and relaxing visibly at the prospect, long powerful thighs spreading.

Rosie was so sleepy and overwhelmed by the events of the day that she would not have cared had he announced that he was taking her to the moon. He had turned her life upside down though: she was very much aware of that. She flexed her crushed toes in the designer shoes she wore, brushed the expensive fabric of her dress with a wondering hand and rested her head back drowsily. It was like being a princess for a day, she thought ruefully, but fine feathers did not make fine birds because underneath she was the exact same Rosie Gray and not at all the sort of woman normally associated with a billionaire. And while enumerating all the possible ways in which she did not fit that frame, Rosie fell asleep.

Alexius almost laughed when he realised that Rosie was dead to the world: a woman had never fallen asleep in his company before. After all, he never spent the night with a woman and while he was awake his normal style of lover was too hyped up with the desire to entertain and impress him to relax to that extent. But then Rosie didn't fall into the normal category for him, he acknowledged absently. She was no star-struck groupie, ready to do anything to please, and he was discovering that he very much liked her ability to treat him as an equal and her lack of awe and subservience.

Rosie awakened only when the helicopter landed and she stumbled groggily onto solid ground again. It was dark but the moonlight illuminated a giant white house set against a dark backdrop. She blinked, not quite sure of what she was seeing, for it was so imposing a building that it looked vaguely like a film set to her. 'Where on earth are we?'

'We're on Banos, the island where I spent my earliest years,' Alexius supplied as outside lights came on to show her a uniformed older man trundling their luggage across an immaculate lawn towards the house.

'An island…and a house like a palace,' she mused, insanely aware of her tousled hair and crumpled dress and scolding herself for being so vain. Had she snored while she was asleep? A school friend had once told her that she had snored on a sleepover. Inwardly, she cringed.

'Can I let him out?' Alexius enquired because Bas was whining and scratching in his carrier.

In answer, Rosie grasped the carrier and undid the door. Bas lurched out like a little drunken dog, struggling to balance on his three good legs against the weight of the cast.

'*Thee mou*, he could wring pity from a stone,' Alexius groaned. 'How long does he need the cast for?'

'Another month…' Rosie was endeavouring not to stare goggle-eyed at the magnificent house with its white weatherboarding and long gracious colonnaded verandah. 'Any minute now I expect Scarlett O'Hara to appear on the front step,' she admitted.

'It was modelled on a Southern plantation house in

the thirties for one of my grandmothers,' Alexius conceded.

Nothing could have more adequately illustrated his illustrious, privileged background, Rosie thought dizzily, than the awe-inspiring sight of the marble hall, ornamented with a huge crystal chandelier, a superb wide staircase, bronze statues and more gilded furniture than Rosie had ever seen outside a museum. She just couldn't imagine anyone actually living in such a grand setting and she swallowed hard when a small group of staff filed out of a rear doorway to greet them.

'Rosie, this is Olympia, my housekeeper,' Alexius informed her. 'Olympia will show you upstairs…'

The stout older woman led Rosie up the sweeping staircase and through double doors to the most massive room that Rosie had ever seen. The four-poster bed was draped in what appeared to be hand-painted silk and the rugs were so elegant and muted in tone that Rosie walked round them rather than across them to peer into the dressing room and bathroom that completed the accommodation. Wow and wow again, she reflected, feeling uniquely undeserving of such overpowering luxury. What had he thought when he saw her humble bedsit? It hadn't frightened him off, she conceded with a sense of satisfaction that surprised her. Her cases arrived and with them a maid, who commenced unpacking them and hanging them up in the fancy dressing room. Feeling light years out of her depth at being waited on, Rosie grabbed up her wash bag and fled into the bathroom to take refuge there. Removing her makeup, which had streaked round her eyes enough to make her groan out loud, she stripped off to use the shower and freshen up. The warm flow of the water revived her somewhat and she made use of the towelling robe available to return to the bedroom. Mercifully, the maid had finished and Rosie finally had the time and the opportunity to more closely examine some of the clothes that had arrived only the day before, for she had had to pack them in a hurry. From a drawer she extracted a slinky pale blue nightdress and put it on, noting that excess fabric puddled round her feet. A knock on the door heralded the appearance of another maid with a tray of food.

Rosie fell on the meal like the original starving woman, not even having realised how hungry she was until the tantalising aromas of beautifully cooked food assailed her nose. Afterwards she looked at herself in the mirror, turned sideways and saw that there was still not the slightest sign that she was pregnant, aside of the noticeable swelling of her previously non-existent boobs, a development that fascinated her. She was still very tired, which she knew was common in early pregnancy, and she clambered into bed, thinking that she ought to rest for the blob's…the baby's sake. At least *he* didn't fake things he didn't feel or tell her only what she wanted to hear. And she didn't need to feel guilty about landing him with her as a house guest either, not in such a giant building. Her mind rattled on and on and on, constantly reverting to thoughts of Alexius, which annoyed her. Was it an infatuation similar to something a teenager would experience? she wondered with a grimace while trying not to wonder what he was doing, what he was thinking and…who *was* Adrianna? Did she have the nerve to ask him? She certainly didn't have the right. Her lack of self-discipline infuriated her: here she was worn-out with her brain buzzing like a bee and she seemed totally incapable of falling asleep.

At two in the morning, having leafed through several magazines to pass the time and even switched on the television to look in vain for an English channel, she got out of bed again. Once more she was hungry, didn't know how, only knew that she was. Bas, who did snore like a little train, was sound asleep on top of a rug and she crept out, not wanting to lug him downstairs with her where he might bark at anything strange and wake people up.

The door at the back of the hall through which the staff had emerged led down a stair to a basement kitchen that would have been adequate for a big hotel. She wondered if Alexius entertained a lot, held fancy dinner parties or *wild* weekends. Strange, he seemed so reserved but in bed he had been anything but. In fact, he had been extraordinarily passionate. She lifted her hands and pressed them to her hot face. 'Stop it, stop torturing me,' she urged her mind.

'Who's torturing you?' Alexius enquired lazily from the doorway.

CHAPTER EIGHT

As ALEXIUS switched on the lights, Rosie whirled round in shock, pale blue silk clinging to her lithe body. 'You couldn't sleep either?'

'No.' Alexius studied her as she opened the doors of the giant double refrigerator to pull out cold meat, which she ate where she stood. 'I gather you're hungry.'

Rosie went red and nodded because her mouth was full. It gave her a most gratuitous opportunity to appraise the full impact of Alexius's raw sexuality, his lean powerful physique sheathed in a pair of worn tight jeans and nothing else. Bare-chested, all that golden skin and rippling muscle on display, he took her breath away and desire swelled deep down inside her. He was badly in need of a shave, for dark stubble covered his lower jaw, framing his beautifully sensual mouth. As if she could sate her sensual response to him with food, she hurriedly helped herself to some cheese.

'Didn't you get a meal earlier?' he enquired politely.

Feeling the blush begin as far down as her chest, Rosie winced and nodded.

'Maybe it's being pregnant,' Alexius suggested lazily, scanning her glowing face framed by her moonlight-pale fall of hair with a growing hunger of his own that had nothing to do with his stomach. He ached for her in the most painful of ways and it brought out primal instincts he hadn't known he possessed.

'Maybe the baby likes protein.'

'Why were you talking to yourself?'

Rosie closed the doors of the refrigerator. 'Just thoughts I was having… I couldn't sleep…'

Like an agile cat, Alexius shifted soundlessly a couple of steps closer. 'Thoughts about me?'

Rosie settled scornful green eyes on him. 'Why on earth would I be thinking about you?'

'Why would I be thinking about you?' Alexius traded, very much in unfamiliar territory because he had never before discussed feelings or thoughts with a woman.

'I'm stressing you out?' Rosie suggested teasingly, trying to kick her brain back into gear, trying not to let her gaze linger on him the way it wanted, *needed* to as if being away from Alexius even for just a few hours left her with a deficit she had to meet.

'*Thee mou*…you're so beautiful, *moli mou*.'

Rosie almost laughed out loud but then she saw his eyes and realised that he meant it, truly believed it at that moment and gratification blossomed inside her. For a long, timeless moment they exchanged a look and her heart began to thump really fast in her chest. A hand closed round her wrist and exerted a gentle tug to draw her closer. *Brain*, she shouted inside her head, heart rate rocketing like an express train, *brain, get back here right this minute*. His hands closed around her waist as he lifted her to him and their mouths clashed with the frantic, feverish longing that powered them both. She tasted him and she couldn't get enough of that taste. *You weren't going to do this*, her brain reminded her at that point. *Shut up*, she told it, fingers delving into luxuriant black hair as she strained against him, her body in an electrifying state of anticipation that she couldn't quell. She kept on kissing him as the ache between her thighs built and thrummed through her like a storm warning.

'I've never stopped wanting you since that night,' Alexius growled, thrusting back the door into the hall and heading for the stairs.

'Was that a complaint?' Rosie asked through swollen lips, thrilled that he had gone on wanting her in spite of his failure to call and the subsequent bombshell of her pregnancy, but all the while knowing that there were other more important things she should be thinking about.

'No. You make me feel *alive* for the first time in years,' Alexius fired back, taking the stairs two at a time with her cradled securely in his arms like a captive. 'I like it, but I don't like it when I can't touch you.'

The admission jerked a tripwire in Rosie's brain. 'We shouldn't be doing this…'

'We haven't done anything *yet*,' Alexius reminded her darkly.

Her hand lifted to trace the frustrated curve of his sensually full mouth while her eyes connected with the hungry urgency of his. The desire, she realised, was a two-way street and the knowledge strengthened her: she was not the only one suffering withdrawal symptoms, feeling weak in the hold of fighting off those unwelcome promptings. She couldn't be near him without wanting to touch him and perfectly understood his frustration at not being able to touch her. He kissed her again, his tongue delving with erotic skill, and the world spun dizzily around her. He dropped her down on a mercifully well-sprung bed in a lamplit room even larger than her own and straight away, separated from that big powerful body of his and the devastating allure of him, she remembered what she had wanted to ask him about.

'Who's Adrianna?'

Engaged in unzipping his jeans, Alexius glanced at her with a frown of surprise. 'Someone I slept with months ago.'

'Not a serious relationship, then?' Rosie pried helplessly.

'I don't do serious.'

Rosie knew that strategy very well, had enjoyed several first dates with men who couldn't relax until they had assured her of the same thing. It had amused her that a man could feel the need to warn her off before either of them even got to know each other, but for some reason it did not amuse her when the same phrase fell so smoothly from Alexius's lips. 'So, why were the journalists asking about her, then?' Rosie persisted doggedly.

'Adrianna gave several interviews to magazines implying that there was more between us than a brief affair. That happens a lot to me with women,' Alexius admitted, coming down on the bed beside her like a naked bronzed god, or at least a massively aroused naked bronzed god.

'Aren't you the popular one? My goodness, it's no wonder you have an ego the size of the sun!' Rosie quipped.

Alexius laughed, the tension in his features roused by her questions vanishing. He didn't always know where he was with her and that was another first for him with a woman. 'Have I?'

'Totally,' Rosie whispered, lying back on his big bed and feeling remarkably like a seductress. It was the way he was looking at her, those light eyes glittering against his brown skin and eating her up as though she were an amazingly desirable creature and she liked the feeling.

'It doesn't impress you, though, does it?'

'No, but I was impressed when you ran up the stairs carrying me,' Rosie told him truthfully, allowing a hand to settle on a broad bronzed shoulder, exulting in the heat and strength of him.

'You don't weigh any more than a child.'

Her sultry mouth down curved. 'I'm going to get fatter and heavier soon.'

'There'll simply be more of you to enjoy, *moraki mou*,' Alexius husked, reaching down for the hem of her nightdress to pull it up and over her head.

'Oh!' Taken by surprise, Rosie crossed her arms over herself. 'Did you plan this when you brought me here?'

Again, Alexius laughed but he picked his words with care. 'Let's say that I entertained the hope that we would get together again.'

Unimpressed, Rosie shook her head. 'I know you—you planned it this way.'

In answer, Alexius shot her a brilliant smile of one-upmanship and crushed her mouth slowly beneath his. Something low in her pelvis clenched, making her hips shift up to him. He uncrossed her hands and directed his lips lower to caress the delicate swell of her breasts and torment the hotly engorged buds that were screamingly sensitive to his attention. As he employed his mouth and his tongue and even his teeth to tease the tender peaks,

Rosie writhed, the simmering heat at the heart of her developing a more desperate edge of need. He absorbed her responses with keen interest, spreading her out on the bed to feast his eyes on, forestalling her every attempt to conceal her body from him.

'I've waited a long time for this,' he protested raggedly, running an admiring forefinger down between her breasts to the pale tangle of curls below, brushing her thighs apart while she held her breath, smoothing over the soft skin of her inner thigh to explore the warm wet invitation of her lush opening. 'And you were definitely worth waiting for, *moraki mou*.'

Trembling, Rosie rested back, scarcely believing what she was allowing, finally acknowledging that she wanted to be with him so much that she didn't care about the terms or the absence of promises. He circled the little pearl of nerve endings that controlled her response and reaction jackknifed through her in an unquenchable surge of charged pleasure. It went on and on and her hips wriggled, her taut nipples abraded by contact with his hair-roughened torso. He sank a finger deep into her and she gasped, her neck arching, slender muscles straining up to the climax she sensed gathering.

'You don't get to come unless I'm inside you,' Alexius spelt out roughly, eyes bright with intensity, already positioning her for his entrance. 'And I'm on a knife edge trying to wait.'

The edge of his desperation racked up her arousal even more. He was almost vibrating with eagerness against her, the muscles in his powerful arms bunched with effort, his jaw line hard as a rock.

'*Don't* wait,' she told him between gritted teeth, her

head rolling restively across the pillow, her body keyed to a frustrating high of expectation.

He filled her to the hilt in one swift motion that stole the breath from her lungs in a gasp. Excitement assailed her as she felt herself stretch to accommodate his size.

'Am I hurting you?' he husked, throwing his handsome head back, black hair wildly tousled by her fingers as he hitched her legs round his waist.

'No, that was a wince of pure pleasure,' she gasped as he sank even deeper into her.

'You're so tight,' he grated with satisfaction, withdrawing almost completely from her body only to thrust back into her tender sheath again, sending goose bumps and tiny hairs prickling all over her skin along with deliriously satisfying sensation. He twisted his hips, changed his angle, and the momentum gathered like a great wave of heat surging through her as he began to thrust into her. The pace quickened. She couldn't breathe, couldn't think, could only *feel* the rampant masculine force of his primal rhythm and the spasms of excitement sent glorious little tremors rippling through her that grew into a blaze of exhilaration that left her moaning and sobbing at the ecstasy of climax. Delight and more delight followed in the melting waves of sheer pleasure that engulfed her. Finally surrendering control, he shuddered above her, his breathing harsh, but the look of appreciation stamped on his face as he gazed down at her was sufficient to tilt her heart inside her.

At her first attempt to move away, Alexius held fast to her, their bodies hot and slippery with sweat and still joined. Finally, he flung himself back against the pillows and arranged her on top of him, arms still holding her close as he kissed her brow, pushed her hair off her face and studied her closely. 'Already I'm thinking about the next time.' He groaned the admission in despair. 'That's what you do to me and it was even more amazing than I remembered, *moraki mou*.'

'Was it? I fell asleep that time.'

Alexius sat up and scrambled off the bed, still holding her. 'Not tonight,' he warned, striding into the bathroom to set her down in the shower and pummel the controls to deluge them both with warm reviving water. 'Tonight I want you over and over and over again.'

'Why?' Rosie asked him baldly.

'Because I'm fed up with wanting you and not having you,' he growled.

Still quivering with sensual aftershocks, Rosie leant against him, sated and momentarily weak. 'I'm here now.'

'And not going anywhere away from me,' Alexius specified with a shot of possessiveness in his veins that lit up warning signs in his shrewd brain, for he had not the slightest idea why, apart from the obvious, it seemed so crucial to keep her close. 'Not for the foreseeable future.'

'You're so bossy sometimes.' Rosie sighed, tingling as he soaped her with shower gel, big hands smoothing slowly and teasingly over her sensitised breasts and down over her still-flat stomach. Before long the exquisite sensitivity engendered by the first bout of their lovemaking awakened every nerve ending to fresh life. She felt his bold shaft hard and full of promise against her and made not the smallest objection when he tipped up her face and hungrily crushed her mouth under his again before he toppled her dripping wet back on the bed, ignoring her laughing protests to cover her body with his again. And if the first time had been wild and exciting the second was slow and deep and almost indescribably satisfying, her body still pulsing with satiation in the aftermath.

Alexius gazed down at her with veiled eyes that silvered with sudden annoyance. She had led him a dance and he didn't like that. Although he had no idea what went on inside her head and had never wanted to know what went on inside a woman's head, his ignorance continually inflamed him when he was with her. And right then, holding her close, his libido mercifully eased by the best sex he had ever had, her small face dreamy and dazed by the same compulsive release, anger suddenly rose uppermost and drove tension through his every muscle. On what grounds had she found him wanting? No woman had ever judged Alexius wanting in any field.

'So I'm good enough to sleep with but not good enough to marry?' he murmured in a lazily provocative but succinct undertone.

Rosie blinked, yanked back with a vengeance from the soothing relaxation of mind-blowing sex. 'It's not that simple,' she mumbled, playing for time, needing her brain to waken from catatonic mode, for being with Alexius seemed to wipe out rational thinking processes.

'It's exactly that simple,' Alexius grated in harsh disagreement.

Picking up on the derisive edge to his accented drawl, Rosie stiffened and, with difficulty because he was so much larger and heavier, pushed him away, no longer easy with the intimacy of lying naked with entwined limbs. She sat up, then grimaced. 'You've already admitted that you don't do serious and marriage is a very serious commitment.'

'It would be different with you. You're having my child,' he pointed out and, without warning, he pressed a hand to her narrow shoulder to push her flat against the pillows again and he splayed a big hand across her stomach. 'That's *my* baby in there.'

Disconcerted by both the gesture and the anger that smouldered in his stunning silver gaze, Rosie wriggled right off the bed and snatched up her nightdress and shimmied into it with frantic hands. 'That doesn't mean you own me.'

'It damn well does!' Alexius suddenly roared at her in rebuttal. 'If you think I'm likely to stand by and watch now while you get involved with another man, you've picked the wrong guy!'

Although she was intimidated by his fury, Rosie lifted her chin and gave him a freezing look. 'It might be your baby but my body is my own and if you had any idea at all of how ordinary people live—which you *don't*—you would appreciate that my chances of meeting another man have been seriously damaged by the simple fact that I'm pregnant!'

'Why should that matter to you? You're my woman. Get used to the fact!' Alexius grated, outraged that she could talk about her chances of meeting another man while still warm from his body, even more enraged that she could even think along such lines.

'I'm not your woman. I'm not any man's woman,' Rosie declared. 'And I'm not hitching my wagon to yours just because you've got a private jet and loads of money! That's not my dream—that's not what I want out of life!'

'What the hell *do* you want from me?' Alexius shot back at her with sizzling incomprehension.

'*Feelings*, you blockhead!' Rosie thundered back at him with incredulity that he had still not got that message. 'It's not enough that you'd be a great provider and fantastic in bed!'

Alexius vaulted off the bed. 'You think I'm going to fall in love with you like some infatuated teenager?' he derided in an all-encompassing rage, driven by exasperation and the belief that she wanted him to provide some fairy-tale solution that he couldn't hope to achieve.

'That's right—mock my dreams!' Rosie hissed, her face red as fire. 'But it doesn't have to be love, just caring, unselfishness, kindness—'

'Haven't I been caring? Haven't I been kind?' Alexius bit out, furious that she was making him defensive.

Rosie thought of his behaviour since she had given him her news and had to acknowledge that he had demonstrated both attributes but she still thought there ought to be more. 'You don't even want our baby.'

'I want you,' Alexius fired back bluntly. 'And I'm starting to think of the baby as a person attached to you. Isn't that enough to start with?'

That he still wanted her, regardless of the baggage she brought with her, meant a great deal to Rosie and she couldn't deny it, but deep down inside her something still said no to the notion of marrying a man who didn't love her, who, whether he would admit it or not, still imagined that his enormous wealth should be sufficient inducement to overcome all other objections.

'I appreciate that you're offering a good deal,' she muttered in an effort she barely understood to placate him, but they had been so close there for a couple of hours and she couldn't bear to feel shut out again. 'Especially to someone like me from a poor background.'

The tension screaming from his stance ebbed and his eyes veiled. 'That doesn't come into the equation. You're one of the kindest and most considerate people I've ever met.'

'That doesn't say much for the people you know.'

'You're not interested in my money. You don't try to take advantage of me and I like being with you. Believe me, those facts matter more,' Alexius delivered curtly. 'But I don't have the emotional capacity to give you love. I've never been in love in my life.'

'Never?' Rosie was shocked.

'It's always been sex for me, nothing more complex,' Alexius acknowledged grudgingly. 'And I like sex more with you than with anyone else.'

Rosie resisted a sudden staggering urge to weep. 'I suppose that's something,' she said shakily, astonished by his claim but strangely touched as well. Indeed, Alexius ignited a whole host of conflicting emotions inside her.

'It's more than something on my terms, *moraki mou*,' Alexius shot back on her.

'That's our most fundamental difference,' Rosie responded ruefully. 'Sex is more important to you, lower on the scale for me. But great sex doesn't mean we'd have a great marriage.'

Condemned for the one bond she was willing to admit that they shared, Alexius felt like punching a wall and instead seethed with silent aggravation. No woman had ever infuriated him so much and it galled him that he felt lost in the dialogue, didn't automatically know the right answers, the perfect angle to take to emerge supreme. He gritted his even teeth and said nothing at all. Rosie unfroze from her self-justifying stance and closed the distance between them. She linked her hands round his neck with difficulty and stretched up to press a kiss to the corner of his unsmiling mouth. 'I don't want to argue with you.'

'But you *are*.'

Rosie ran a frankly manipulative hand down over his bronzed, hair-roughened torso, revelling in the heat and muscularity of his strong physique, and pressed as close as she dared to mutter shamefacedly, because she knew she was taking the easy way out, 'Let's go back to bed...'

Relief assailed Alexius. Lust he understood in the same way that he understood that he needed air to breathe. It was honest and offered no room for misunderstandings. He carried her small hand lower.

'Remember asking me for directions?' he remarked not quite steadily, startled at the speed with which his erection returned at the first shy brush of her fingers. He was accustomed to everything but ignorance in the bedroom. A long line of very experienced eager-to-please sophisticates had given him high expectations of his lovers, but nothing had ever excited him as much as Rosie's hesitant overture at that moment. And that was in spite of the fact that he knew exactly what she was doing in smoothing over the discomfiture roused by the conversation *he* should never have started.

Rosie skimmed tentative fingers down his hard, thick shaft and shed the turmoil of thoughts torturing her. What was right? What was wrong? Did it really matter as long as she was happy?

And happiness was humming through Rosie when she opened her eyes the following morning: Alexius was there, mere inches away, and his presence soothed her. His lean, hard-boned face was softer in slumber, his outrageously long black lashes almost hitting his exotic cheekbones. So good-looking, so vital, so full of mystery. She wanted to get under his skin, grasp why he was so reserved, learn if he was hiding anything, *sort him out* like a challenging jigsaw puzzle. But then he fascinated her and after the night of unashamed passion they had shared she didn't think her response to him was likely to change any time soon. She ached but it was a pleasurable ache of passion shared and rejoiced in. He was amazing in bed, would probably be highly insulted if he ever found out that for her the best part was being held afterwards, feeling so physically close and valued, her heart lifting when he smiled or laughed.

It scared her that he could already have so much power over her. She hadn't consciously made the choice to give that power to him, yet somehow he had taken it, stealing her heart the first chance he got. She had fallen for him so easily but he was never going to love her back: that was very clear. When she thought of the many female options he must always have available, she knew it would be banging her head up against a brick wall to hope for more. She was a novelty to Alexius Stavroulakis, she decided uneasily, an ordinary working woman who had been a virgin. Of course she was different from his previous lovers, but for how long would her novelty value exercise this amount of pulling power over him? If she wasn't careful she could easily slip into the trap of just wanting to make Alexius happy. She could hardly have failed to have noticed that happiness when he laughed or smiled always seemed to take him by surprise.

They had a long, leisurely breakfast on the verandah overlooking the beach—a long strip of almost-white sand washed by the murmuring surf below a crystalline-blue clear sky. The amazing view was worthy of the equally amazing house, which he had shown her over before they ate. It was big but still stuck in the time band in which it had been built as if nobody had ever stayed there long enough to bother updating or personalising it, and she had looked in vain for family photos.

'We weren't that kind of family,' Alexius had commented wryly.

'But it must have been terrific fun living here when you were a kid with the beach right on the doorstep.'

Alexius had said nothing and the silence had been uncomfortable.

Curiosity had thrummed through Rosie. 'You didn't have much fun as a kid, did you?'

'No,' he had finally conceded. 'But I was very well educated and looked after,' he had asserted, lest she receive some image of neglect from his words. 'Let's go for a walk…'

The walk on the beach killed that topic of conversation, which she rather thought had been his objective. Rosie was strolling dreamily through the cooling surf when Alexius got a phone call on his mobile. He spoke in Greek and smiled before leaning back against a rock to continue the call while extending a hand to Rosie to draw her back to him and pull her under his arm. It was that sort of gesture that gave her hope that he *did* care, maybe more than he knew, for he definitely liked to stay in physical contact even outside the bedroom door. She buried her nose in his shirtfront, loving the sun-warmed already-familiar smell of his clothing and his body, the reassuring thump of his heartbeat below her cheek and the very fact that he was simply holding her. It wasn't sex, after all, she reasoned—he didn't *have* to hold her. After what seemed like a fairly lengthy chat, Alexius came off the phone again.

'Your grandfather is flying in to see you this afternoon,' he told her.

Rosie was torn between pleasure and concern. 'Why?'

'Obviously to mend fences with you!' Alexius groaned. 'You're his granddaughter. That means a lot to a man with his family history.'

'I don't want him leaning on me to marry you again,' Rosie confided uneasily. 'So, I hope that's not why he's coming here.'

'I've withdrawn the offer,' Alexius told her without skipping a beat. 'You're right. Why should we get married? We're having *amazing* sex. I'm content with that.'

Rosie discovered that she was far from predictable because, instead of relaxing now that the source of that pressure had gone, she was torn between wanting to scream and wanting to slap him. He'd withdrawn his marriage proposal? *He* was content? Well, she blasted well wasn't! Had he changed his mind because she had fallen into bed with him again? It was a mortifying suspicion. Just then she felt as if she was lost in an emotional no-man's-land, wanting and needing him and yet reluctant to admit to either sentiment and fearful of the likely outcome to such vulnerability.

* * *

Socrates Seferis was seated in a wicker chair on the verandah enjoying coffee and tiny pastries when Rosie came downstairs to join him, freshly garbed in linen trousers and a bright blue tee. Her smile was hesitant. 'I'm so pleased you wanted to see me again,' she admitted frankly.

'You and Alexius are adults. I shouldn't have interfered and sitting on the sidelines like this…' the older man smiled widely '…is proving very interesting.'

Rosie poured a cold drink from the tray on the table. 'How…interesting?'

'My godson has never brought a woman here before. This island is his bolthole. He is very protective of his privacy.'

'I'm not surprised. I saw how the press behaved around him at the airport. Not a fun experience.' Rosie winced at the recollection but she wanted to smile at the information her grandfather had just given her. It was good to know that she was not one more in a long line of female lovers brought to Alexius's childhood home. 'Have you been here before?'

'Only once. His parents' funeral,' Socrates volunteered wryly. 'They are interred in the private cemetery here.'

Her interest caught, Rosie leant forward. 'You *knew* them? What were they like?'

'I never moved in their elite social circle, consequently I can really only speak as an observer,' the older man confessed. 'I went to school with Alexius's grandfather and that was my connection to his family and why I was asked to be Alexius's godfather. His parents were both very rich and very young. They were also only children whose families pushed them together and their marriage was more or less a business merger. Once their families were satisfied by the production of a son and heir—Alexius—his parents lived separate lives. There was no divorce but there was no true marriage either.'

Rosie nodded. 'That's sad.'

'But rather more sad for their son,' Socrates countered ruefully. 'I think his mother lacked the maternal instinct. Alexius was raised by the domestic staff and at the age of eight his parents placed him in an English boarding school.'

'Eight years old? That's very young to be sent so far from home, but no wonder he speaks such good English,' Rosie mused, riveted by what she was learning. 'He never mentions his childhood.'

'Let me tell you a story,' Socrates urged, sprawling comfortably back in his padded wicker chair. 'Once I was in London on a business trip when I suddenly remembered that it was my godson's tenth birthday. I'm an impulsive man and since I hadn't seen the boy in quite a while I decided to buy him a gift and pay him a surprise visit at the school. When I arrived I was taken aside by his housemaster, who confided that the school was very concerned by the boy's lack of contact with family and home. He never heard from his parents at all and they didn't bother to visit even if they were in the UK. Summers he spent here on the island but as a rule neither parent was present, only the staff, who catered to his every whim. Alexius never learned what a normal family household was like because he never had that experience.'

Rosie was pale, imagining how lonely he must have been as a child, given everything necessary for his comfort and amusement but deprived entirely of parental love, interest and attention. 'That must have been very wounding for him.'

Socrates elevated a bushy greying brow. 'He'll never admit that, but once I knew that he had no visitors at school I made it my business to see him whenever I was in London. He had plenty of friends, of course, and often visited their homes.'

Rosie sank into a reflective mood, grasping that she finally had the key to her lover's essential detachment. Just like her he had been betrayed and excluded by the people who should have loved him and wanted to keep him close as a child. Great wealth might have shielded him from the early deprivations she had experienced, but, regardless, his mistreatment had been no less real than her own.

'Would you like to come and stay with me in my home in Athens?' her grandfather asked her baldly without the smallest warning. 'You'd be very welcome.'

Rosie reddened and shifted in her seat, mortified by her reluctance, for she could now see that the older man was a warm-hearted person, willing to move past his own views of her current pregnant and unwed condition purely to build a family relationship with her. 'I…er—'

'Don't want to leave Alexius,' he slotted in, a glint of amusement in his dark eyes. 'So, you *are* a couple?'

'Right now…I'd like to spend more time with him,' Rosie admitted in a rush, her colour higher than ever at being put on the spot to quantify something she couldn't even begin to describe.

'My invitation remains open. I would love to have you as a guest and I'd like to hold a party to introduce you to my friends and relatives,' Socrates declared with enthusiasm. 'But that can wait.'

'I'm grateful that you understand,' Rosie responded guiltily, for hadn't she originally agreed to come to Greece to get to know her grandfather? When had she allowed Alexius to become the sole focus of her happiness and her dreams?

Socrates Seferis shook his head slowly. 'I don't understand why you won't marry him…feeling as you so obviously do about him,' he confided equally. 'But you're old enough to know your own business best.'

After that slightly awkward exchange, Socrates told her about his problems with his own family and she admired his honesty and respected his wry admission that he had spoiled and indulged his children in an attempt to compensate them for the death of their mother. He moved on to discuss the fact that he had asked Alexius to get to know her and Rosie then told her grandfather about his godson's deception, which the older man found surprisingly funny.

Alexius strolled lithely out to join them and mention that dinner would soon be served. Clad in an open shirt with every sleek muscular line of his body defined by cropped denim jeans, he took her breath away. She was amused to see Bas stumbling along in his wake, little tail wagging like a metronome as soon as he saw Rosie. She lifted the little dog onto her knee and introduced him to her grandfather.

'He followed me into my bedroom and started chewing one of my shoes,' Alexius delivered grimly, choosing not to admit that he had been relieved that his ankle was not the target again.

'He does have bad habits. He wasn't very well trained when he was a puppy,' Rosie explained.

'You spoil him. He's an animal, not a human being.'

'Well, I'm sorry about the shoe but I'm not putting him outside in a kennel!' Rosie told him squarely.

Socrates watched the exchange as if he were in the front seat viewing an enthralling show and, catching him in the act, Rosie flushed with self-consciousness, wondering if she and Alexius looked as ill suited from the outside as she felt they had to be. Never mind his wretched money and pedigreed background, she thought painfully, he was so damned clever while she was always aware that she had to study long and hard to pass exams.

After dinner the two men chatted with an ease that relieved her fear that their confrontation on the day of her arrival had caused lasting damage to their relationship. The helicopter arrived to collect her grandfather and convey him home. She walked back indoors by Alexius's side, suddenly shy again, tied in knots by the potential pitfalls of a relationship that had no boundaries or definition.

'Did Socrates ask you to go home with him?' Alexius asked darkly, scrutinising the shuttered look of her delicate profile with suspicion while noting the faint sunburn that had already turned her cheekbones pink, and lingering on the lush pout of her soft mouth.

Rosie lifted her head, pale hair falling back from her brow, her eyes evasive. 'Yes.'

Alexius tensed. 'And what did you say?'

'Not just yet.' Rosie swallowed, feeling like a shameless hussy for admitting that so openly, for obviously she had no reason to stay other than to share his bed.

His wide sensual mouth narrowed thoughtfully. 'That's good.'

'However, I do intend to take him up on the invite soon,' Rosie continued doggedly, keen to let him know that he was not saddled with her as a house guest in an open-ended arrangement. 'I'm sure you'll be jetting off somewhere soon to work.'

Alexius had come to a halt, his face taut, his eyes shielded. 'I'm planning to take some time off. How soon is soon?' he queried.

'A…week?' Rosie tested the concept on him uncertainly. 'I don't feel I can put my grandfather off much longer than that. After all, I did come to Greece to spend time with him and here I am staying with you.'

Alexius ran a teasing forefinger below her full lower lip that made her tingle, and she glanced up into his mesmerising eyes, liquid heat spiralling between her slender thighs. 'A week isn't long enough for what I want, *moraki mou*.'

'This…*us*,' she specified unevenly, 'isn't going anywhere.'

Alexius scooped her up in his arms, ignoring Bas, who was bouncing round their legs and barking at the move. 'Right now, we're going to bed.'

Sex, his first port of call, his main means of self-expression, she thought despairingly even as the wild excitement of his hungry mouth on hers and his arms crushing her to him leapt like a burning flame to her every pulse point. Sex, shorn of emotion, was the lowest possible denominator. But did that matter if she wanted to be with him more than anything else in the world? She shrugged off her doubts and insecurity, and reminded herself that she had turned down a marriage that would have tied him to her whether he liked it or not. She didn't want to become the wife he felt duty bound to marry because she was carrying his child. Eventually, he would come to resent her for such a sacrifice. No, what little they had now was still more honest and true than a second-rate marriage would have been, she told herself urgently, for one truth she had divined: Alexius Stavroulakis was constitutionally incapable of accepting *anything* second-rate.

CHAPTER NINE

WHEN are you going to tell Alexius? was the question running on a constant loop inside Rosie's head. Tell him that she was *leaving* tomorrow? Her grandfather had already arranged transport for her and set the date of the promised party for the weekend.

It wasn't even as though her departure could be much of a surprise to Alexius, she reasoned ruefully, because the one week she had conceded at the start had stretched languorously into two weeks. Only the onset of Socrates's regular phone calls had persuaded her to finally set a date. He was her grandfather, a man she liked and respected, and she knew very well that he was only thinking about her well-being. Letting the precious days trickle through her fingers like a dream she was frantically struggling to hold on to against all the odds wasn't adult behaviour, she told herself urgently. She was pregnant; she couldn't afford to drift for ever. She had to make a new life for the sake of her child and her grandfather was offering her the first stepping stone towards that sensible objective. She had stayed with Alexius because she had hoped against hope that he would show feelings for her that went beyond what they shared in bed.

Sadly, it hadn't happened. Nor had he mentioned the marriage idea since the day he told her that he was withdrawing that offer, which implied that he had come round to her point of view and accepted that marriage wasn't for him. His silence was deeply ironic at a time when Rosie was revising *her* convictions and beginning to believe that a good marriage could possibly be built on something other than mutual devotion. Alexius was *so* good to her: no man had ever treated Rosie so well and when it was happening on a daily basis she knew it was worthy of note.

They had explored the island together, bathed off idyllic deserted beaches and eaten out at the homely *taverna* in the dusty little village down by the harbour, where the local fishermen wandered up to chat to Alexius with a lack of concern for his exalted tycoon status that she knew he relished. He had no need of bodyguards on the island, which was why he so enjoyed his freedom there. He had even taken her out fishing, but that had been a calamity as the motion of the boat and the smell of the fish had made her unrelentingly sick. To console her for her weakness he had flown her to Rhodes the next day, amused when she was less interested in the shops than in touring the medieval walled city and learning its chequered history, but even so he had still contrived to buy her a spectacular diamond pendant at an exclusive jeweller's that had proved the source of their only row during their time together.

'I'll give you whatever I want!' Alexius had retorted angrily, refusing to compromise when she told him she was uncomfortable accepting such an expensive gift. 'You're sleeping in my bed, you're expecting my baby— why do you expect me to treat you like a casual acquaintance? And what's your problem anyway? Everything you're wearing right down to the panties I'm looking forward to ripping off you later was bought by me!'

That unwelcome truth had landed like a concrete brick on Rosie's proud head, crushing her, embarrassing her, infuriating her for, predictably, Alexius was never slow to deliver the ultimate verbal strike in a clash of personalities. But he *had* apologised, she reminded herself in consolation, even when she hadn't expected him to apologise for only pointing out the truth.

'Don't make my money a barrier between us,' he had urged that night in bed while he held her close, after an explosive bout of passionate make-up sex. 'Don't deny me the pleasure of buying things for you. I don't like rejection.'

She was so happy with him, she acknowledged painfully, but she absolutely knew that returning to Athens to move in with her grandfather would translate as a rejection in Alexius's judgemental eyes. He was very much an all-or-nothing personality. Even so, it wasn't as if Alexius had *asked* her to live with him: if he had asked she would have said yes. But the point was that he *hadn't* asked. Their stay on the island appeared to be more like a little break from routine on his terms and yet it had meant so much more to her.

Rosie folded another top and laid it in the suitcase with a sigh. He hadn't asked her to fall in love with him. In fact, had he known he would undoubtedly have told her not to bother doing so. She remembered that Bas's lead and his toys were downstairs and went to fetch them. As usual Alexius had spent the morning working in his home office and she had not seen him since breakfast. She was digging out a squeaky toy from below a table when he appeared.

'I've done enough for one day, *moraki mou*,' he mused, lounging in the doorway, black hair tousled, bronzed muscular torso on show below an open shirt worn with swimming trunks. Even dressed that casually, he exuded a throbbing, energising aura of power and temperament, a slight smile curving his beautifully moulded lips. As she looked her mouth went dry, her breath hitched in her throat and her heart lurched: he looked so gorgeous she could never believe that he could be hers in any lasting way. She always had the uneasy feeling that she was reaching for a guy light years out of her reach.

'What are you doing scrabbling about the floor like that?' he enquired levelly.

'Finding Bas's toys,' she muttered, rising upright again to gaze back at him with wide green eyes of appreciation. Oh, how much *more* appreciative she would be tomorrow when she left the island, she conceded painfully, and Alexius would no longer be available. The prospect depressed her.

'Tell the staff to find them,' Alexius urged with the careless ease of a male who never did anything pedestrian that could be done by an employee. He focused his talents and time on business and on being a breathtakingly inventive and exciting lover.

At that risqué thought, her breasts tingled beneath her simple sundress, the bodice a little tight since pregnancy had swelled her flat chest to acceptable curves for the first time in her life. That new fullness of flesh there amused her, for it was only a temporary effect, but the reality that she was losing her waist and could no longer suck her slightly protruding stomach in did not amuse her at all. The body that Alexius swore he adored was changing and there was nothing she could do to stop that from happening. Soon Alexius might not even want to rip her panties off any more because she was losing her figure. Wasn't it better to leave before his desire waned when at least that way she could conserve her pride? After all, pride was all a girl had left when she loved a man who didn't feel the same way.

Alexius sensed her edginess and noticed the way her eyes dropped from his. He had known there was something amiss for the past forty-eight hours but had said nothing, holding back as was his wont from the lifelong awareness that that was the best way to hang on to power in any relationship. But something or someone had definitely robbed Rosie of her ever-present delight in life. She had a tremendous capacity for joy and more inclination to admire, appreciate and value the little things of life than he had ever met with in any other person, Alexius reflected with unabated wonderment. A beautiful sunset, a delicious meal or even a lame joke from an old fisherman could inspire her to smiles and laughter: she was cheerful, easy to please, and she had finally learned to accept his limits. She was the perfect lover.

'Are you feeling all right?' Alexius asked abruptly, surprising himself with that leading question, but her nervousness nagged at him like a sore tooth. And not for nothing had Alexius devoured whole a thoroughly depressing book entitled Pregnancy Disasters. He knew exactly what danger signs to look out for and silently checked her every day for any suspicious symptom or visible and dangerous alteration.

Rosie smiled, determined not to spoil their last day together. 'Of course I am.'

Alexius trailed long fingers through the tumbled fall of her hair across her shoulders, enjoying the familiar scent of her herbal shampoo. A cascade of images gripped him: Rosie grinning with enthusiasm with her hair blowing wildly back from her face on the boat, enjoying herself before the sickness bug took over; Rosie studying him in the morning as though he were the eighth wonder of the world; Rosie looking at him at all times of day as though he were the eighth wonder of the world, he repeated mentally as he met her dreamy green eyes full-on. He didn't trade in dreams: when would she realise that? But he was content with what they had, wanted to stop the clock right there and then as she shifted into his arms without any prompting and offered her succulent mouth up to his.

He was a great kisser and he kissed her breathless, driving his hunger through her until it became a piercingly sweet arrow of need that provoked moisture between her legs. Hot and damp, she squirmed against him, sighing with pleasure as she felt the hard prod of his arousal against her. He clamped his arms round her and lifted her and she laughed. Bas danced round their feet, begging for attention on their passage to the stairs because he couldn't climb them with his cast and he knew it.

'Bad timing, Bas,' Alexius pronounced raggedly, one hand already prying her slender thighs apart below her dress to discover that she was as eager for him as he was for her. He had never had that with a woman before, that instant sexual connection no matter when or how he touched her, no matter what time of day it was, no matter what mood she was in… It was a priceless quality for a highly sexed male to find in a partner.

He cannoned into her door because he was still kissing her and Rosie giggled as he stumbled and almost fell into her bedroom. She framed his cheeks with adoring hands and collided with stunning silvery eyes that mesmerised her. 'I love your eyes… Did I ever tell you that?'

'Maybe once or twice.' Colour scored his high cheekbones and then he espied the suitcase lying open on the bed and he dumped her down beside it. 'What the hell's this?' he demanded with staggering abruptness.

Rosie snatched in a startled breath. 'I was going to tell you over dinner. Socrates is sending a helicopter to pick me up tomorrow morning.'

Alexius's face was hard as granite. 'And when will you be coming back?'

Rosie slid upright. Her shoes had fallen off downstairs and she hastily smoothed down the skirt of her dress, which had rucked up round her waist. 'I'm going to stay with him, Alexius…like I promised I would.'

Alexius froze into an iceberg in front of her, silver eyes darkening, hardening. 'So, you're walking out on me.'

Dismay filled Rosie. 'No, that's not how it is. You know it's not. He's organised a party for me on Saturday night…won't you be coming to that?'

'This is the first I'd heard of it. When will you be back here?'

Rosie breathed in slow and deep. 'We can't go on this way indefinitely,' she muttered awkwardly, desperate to find and use the right words while knowing she didn't have them in her vocabulary.

'Why not?' Alexius grated harshly.

'Because I have to make plans and I need to take this opportunity to get to know Socrates. I've never had a relative interested in me before—it means a great deal to me, but he's not a young man any more, Alexius. Who knows how long he'll be there for me to be with him?' she appealed, her green eyes deeply troubled. 'Don't make it difficult for me to do what my conscience tells me I have to do.'

'I have no intention of doing so, but if you walk out of this house, it's over between us. I'll support you and my child but I'll move on with my life without you.'

'I know you're annoyed with me, I know I should've discussed this with you first, but you're not being fair!' Rosie cried, panic taking hold of her in a great dizzy surge that made her tummy roil as if she were back in the boat on the sea again. 'You can still see me in Athens—'

'And sleep with you? I don't think so,' Alexius derided. 'Once Socrates has you under his roof, you'll be reinvented as a vestal virgin.'

'A *pregnant* vestal virgin?' Rosie scorned with a jerky little laugh, horribly hurt that he had mentioned nothing but a need for her body. 'Is that a joke? You don't really mean that it's over between us, do you?'

'I do,' Alexius confirmed with icy restraint, the strong bones of his darkly handsome face set in uncompromising lines of resolve. 'I very rarely say things I don't mean, Rosie. If you leave without my permission, we're done for all time.'

'I think, at least I *hope*, you mean agreement rather than permission,' Rosie interrupted sickly. 'Because I don't need your permission for anything.'

Alexius shot her a glittering glance of smouldering hostility. 'You're right. You don't.'

And with that somehow sobering concession for she would have preferred an argument, Alexius strode back out of the room. Rosie sank down on the edge of the bed like a sleepwalker suddenly waking up to find herself in a strange place. A very strange place indeed, she adjusted shakily, anguish threatening to consume her alive. He didn't mean it. He *couldn't* mean it. They could not be over when only minutes earlier he had been ready to make love to her. He couldn't simply switch off like that... Could he?

Over. She tasted the concept and retreated from it again with a shudder. He was angry; he wouldn't stay angry for ever. Her heart still told her that she owed Socrates her attention but her heart was also ready to split right down the middle at the challenging prospect of Alexius dumping her cold. He was acting like a bully. He was too used to always getting what he wanted. He was behaving badly, using emotional blackmail to hit her where it hurt, she thought with pained resentment. And if she was weak, his cruelty would work, but she was not weak. She had to fight him, stick to her guns. He would come round; he *had* to come round. She loved him, she loved him even when he was acting like an absolute four-letter word and lashing out at her. But she should have prepared the ground better, talked over her plans with him, not issued a blunt announcement when he was least in the mood to hear it. The sight of her half-packed suitcase had been a red rag to a bull.

Over—what if he truly meant it? Well, if he did, he was no loss, Rosie reasoned wretchedly, tears pushing past her squeezed-closed eyes as she struggled to hold them back. She was not about to cry and grieve over a guy who issued ultimatums as if she were one of his humble employees! She was strong, she could get by without him, enjoy life *without him*. She might feel as if she couldn't but such a belief was melodramatic nonsense.

CHAPTER TEN

'THERE'S Alexius now,' Rosie's aunt Sofia carolled in Rosie's ear. 'I *told* you he'd be here! He never misses one of Dad's parties.'

Rosie focused her attention on the noticeable crush that had formed on the far side of the room. She could only see the top of Alexius's arrogant dark head because he was taller than the men around him. Perspiration beaded her short upper lip and her hands clenched in on themselves. A full week had passed since she had left the island and Alexius had not got in touch once. Not once! Keeping her distance from him demanded every ounce of her self-control and she wondered why that was so when he was the one behaving badly. What had happened to her pride? 'Who are all those people with him?' she asked, unable to suppress her curiosity.

'Alexius always gets mobbed in public. He's a very powerful man in business. The men want a piece of what he's got and the women want a piece of *him*,' the older woman spelt out with a suggestive chuckle.

Socrates had chosen to throw his party in his flagship city hotel and had insisted on buying Rosie a new dress for the occasion even though she had shown him an outfit that she had been convinced would do. Had it not been for the emotional turmoil she had suffered in leaving Alexius, she would have thoroughly enjoyed the week she had spent in her grandfather's company. On his home turf, Rosie and Socrates had relaxed and developed a close bond, discovering a very similar sense of humour and an equally strong appreciation of unpretentious living.

Rosie was wearing white, which nicely set off the light golden tan she had acquired on the beach, and she had had her hair done specially for the occasion, so that the pale strands fell waterfall straight past her shoulders. The dress was more revealing than what she was accustomed to wearing though, and she felt wildly self-conscious in it. Sofia had taken Rosie shopping, however, and saying no to the ebullient Sofia was no easy task. Rosie thought that she and her aunt were too different to ever be close, but Sofia had curbed her waspish tongue since Rosie's arrival and the older woman's blunt opinions were, admittedly, informative and often amusing. The older woman knew everyone who was anyone in society and was thoroughly acquainted with every scandal and secret worth hearing about. Rosie was convinced that all the guests must already know that she was pregnant and by whom for she could not believe that Sofia was capable of keeping such a juicy piece of gossip to herself.

'Who's she?' Rosie prompted, dry-mouthed, as a gap in the crowd round Alexius revealed a glimpse of a striking brunette in a bright blue skimpy dress with a possessive hand locked to the father of her child's arm. Yes, that was right, Rosie reminded herself vitriolically, he *was* the father of her child and it was cheap and tasteless of Alexius to be showing off another woman at her party.

'Yannina Demas...Demas Shipping,' Sofia extended authoritatively. 'They're old friends, but Nina has always wanted more. Don't stare at him, Rosie. Never wear your heart on your sleeve for a man, particularly not one with so many options available.'

Instantly, Rosie turned her pale head away, flags of stricken colour mantling her cheeks as if she had been slapped. Was she that transparent? Were her feelings for Alexius so obvious? She could hardly eat and she certainly wasn't sleeping. Undeniably her spirits were low. With each day that had dragged past without a visit or even a casual phone call, Rosie had suffered more as she struggled to keep her feelings under control. At one point she had almost got desperate enough to phone Alexius and tell him not to be so stupid but had managed to restrain herself from such a revealing act. *Old friends?* Former bed partners or genuine old friends? Nina Demas was clinging to Alexius as though he were her only support in a violent storm. Rosie blanked the view and suppressed the thought to smile at the tall young man asking her to dance.

Alexius watched Rosie walk onto the dance floor: she looked disorientatingly unfamiliar. That dress had certainly not come from the conservative wardrobe he had ordered for her. It was very short with a fitted bodice that bared her shoulders and showcased her breasts, while the skirt sat out below her waist decorated with fluffy flowers of fabric. Once she would have dismissed such a very feminine dress as silly and frivolous but the whole effect was stunning and sophisticated and it stood for all the qualities Alexius had never wanted Rosie to acquire.

He had liked her simplicity, her unashamed lack of glamour and vanity. He didn't like her putting her pregnancy-enhanced breasts on display or showing off her slender, shapely legs, which would only encourage men to wonder what it would be like to lie between them. If it weren't for the salient little fact that he had ditched her, Alexius would have rushed over there and wrapped his jacket round Rosie to shield her from the clothes-stripping male eyes locked to her because she was attracting far too much attention. And Alexius didn't like that either. Even less did he like the way she was behaving as he watched her slender hips swivelling in time to the music in a sexually provocative display. What the hell did she think she was playing at? His temper smouldered like boiling oil below the polite social smile he wore in response to a sally from Nina.

Rosie's aunt spoke to her as she came off the floor to say, 'If you can spare five minutes, Dad wants to see you upstairs in his suite.'

Breathing audibly from her efforts on the dance floor, Rosie entered the lift that would take her up to Socrates's private suite. She wondered if something had happened and worried that the older man had been doing too much and wasn't feeling well. Taking adequate rest was a challenge for a man as energetic as Socrates Seferis, who was very much a hands-on employer. The door of the suite stood ajar and she walked on in, glancing round, surprised to find herself alone. A moment later, the door opened wide and Alexius strode in impatiently, wheeling to a surprised halt when he saw her standing there.

'Socrates?'

'He's not here yet,' Rosie proclaimed stiffly, clash-
ing unwarily with liquid mercury eyes set between lush
black lashes, her mouth running dry. Alexius looked
spectacular in his formal suit, his skin like polished
bronze against his white shirt collar, his lean, strong
face outrageously handsome but clenched in hard, taut
lines. 'Did he want to speak to you as well?'

'Right now it looks more like he wanted *us* to speak
to each other,' Alexius responded with a cynical smile
as he closed the door, sealing them into unwelcome
privacy.

Rosie froze. 'I've got nothing to say to you.'

'That's fine because I've got plenty to say!' Alexius
retorted harshly, studying the slim figure shamelessly
exposed in the figure-hugging dress, his wide sensual
mouth twisting with derision. Her newly plump breasts
pouted delectably in the neckline and as he helplessly
pictured the taut little berries of her nipples a heavy
ache stirred with aggravating intensity at his groin.
'What are you doing coming out in public dressed like
that?'

'Like what?' Rosie demanded defiantly, intimidated
against her will by the sheer imposing size of him standing within a few feet of her while her mind was bom-
barded with intimate images she had buried deep:
Alexius setting her on fire with his clever hands and
even more erotic mouth; Alexius driving her wild from
dawn to dusk, his hunger for her knowing no bounds.
'What's wrong with the way I'm dressed?'

'You're showing far too much flesh for a pregnant
woman,' Alexius declared without hesitation. 'It's indecent.'

'I don't look pregnant yet!' Rosie flung back at him furiously, wondering if her no longer perfectly flat stomach was visible and all stirred up by the suspicion that she might be looking rather ridiculous.

'But you *are* pregnant,' Alexius reminded her with something very much like satisfaction. 'And throwing yourself about the dance floor in your condition isn't sensible.'

'What would you know about it?' Rosie snapped, mortified by that cutting description of her behaviour. 'We've never danced together and doesn't that say all there is to know about us? We've never danced. We've never had a first date.'

Frustration assailed Alexius. 'It's a little late in the day to worry about that.'

'I hate you!' Rosie launched at him, having failed to get a rise out of him with what to her was a very salient point. 'You're trying to lay down the law and you've got no right. What I wear and how I behave is none of your business!'

'But the baby will always be my business,' Alexius reminded her succinctly. 'Of course you don't hate me.'

'How do you know? You *dumped* me!' Rosie spat back at him with tempestuous bitterness. 'Did you think that was good for me and the baby? And what about all that sex?'

'We enjoyed each other,' Alexius pronounced with supreme assurance, studying the lush pout of her mouth with diamond-bright eyes. 'You had no complaints at the time.'

His intense gaze set her on fire inside her dress, tightening her nipples, causing a surge of moist heat between her thighs so that she pressed them together.

Unbearable hunger pulsed through her slim body and her hands clenched into defensive fists. He reached for her with casual cool, lean fingers closing round her wrists to tug her close.

'No!' Rosie yelled at him fiercely, terrified of being touched and giving him the response he no longer had the right to claim.

But his mouth still ravished hers in a taste of heaven and hell. The heaven was the sweet flood of revitalising longing he released and the hell was her inability to suppress her response. His tongue delved deep and made her shudder violently. He hauled her up against his big powerful body, crushing her tender breasts against his muscular chest while his hands slid beneath her skirt to curve to her slender thighs, parting them as he lifted her to clamp them round his waist.

'What the heck are you playing at?' Rosie condemned, entrapped by his strength and what she saw as her mental weakness.

'I want you…you want me, *moraki mou*. It's that basic,' Alexius growled against her swollen mouth. 'Come home with me now.'

'No way. We're over—you made that clear.'

'I wasn't thinking clearly,' Alexius grated. 'You took me by surprise and then you flounced off before I could do anything about it!'

'Put me down!' Rosie shouted at him, desperate to break free of her terrifying longing to cling to him. 'I left you a week ago and you've done nothing…you didn't even phone!'

Alexius stared down at her, his light eyes reflective. 'I thought you would phone me.'

It was true: he *had* thought that after a little breathing

space she would phone him. She was such a chatterbox, always had a thousand things she wanted to share with him. He had assumed she would not be able to resist the temptation to speak to him and he had resented her silence almost as much as her absence.

With a determined flex of her inner thigh muscles, Rosie contrived to loosen his hold and shimmy down the length of him, although not without discovering the potent thrust of his arousal and gritting her teeth on the thought that only sex could motivate Alexius to such a demonstration. She broke away from him with enraged green eyes. 'How dare you ask me to come home with you?'

'That's where you belong—in my home with me,' Alexius informed her.

'You dumped me!' Rosie shrieked at him again.

Alexius winced at her shrillness. 'I want you back. Back in my home, back in my bed, back with me.'

'It's not going to happen!' Rosie raked back at him in a blazing temper as she stalked to the door and wrenched it open. 'You had your chance and you blew it!'

Alexius was indignant. He was willing to make amends, willing to talk, but he was not about to grovel for a hearing. Yes, he had made mistakes but so had she.

As the lift doors opened her grandfather stepped out. 'Did you talk to Alexius?' he pressed.

'So, you did set us up?' Rosie queried.

'Anything was preferable to watching the two of you acting like sulking teenagers on opposite sides of the room,' Socrates admitted.

'We argued,' Rosie told him grudgingly.

Alexius stepped past Socrates into the lift before the

doors could close again. 'But go ahead and announce our engagement this evening. I have every intention of ensuring that we work out our differences.'

'Announce…*what*? An engagement? Are you crazy? I have no desire to work at anything with you!' Rosie shouted at him full-tilt as she followed him into the lift, outraged at his declaration.

'Did I say I was giving you a choice?' Alexius asked tight-lipped.

'And how do you intend to make me listen?' Rosie hurled. 'Do you ever listen to yourself?'

'Do you ever know when to shut up?' Alexius traded. 'Do you even know why you're arguing with me?'

'You dumped me…I hate you,' Rosie responded without even having to think about it as the lift doors sprang open again.

'You'll get over it,' Alexius asserted, pouncing on her without warning to swing her up into his arms and head first over one shoulder, one hand splayed to the pert curve of her behind to lock her safely in place. 'You're coming home with me now.'

'No, I darned well am not! Put me down right this minute!' Rosie gasped in ringing disbelief as he strode across the foyer towards the exit with everybody staring at them. As her upside-down face burned crimson with embarrassment her fists battered at his broad back in furious frustration. 'I won't tell you again, Alex—put me down!'

'You should know by now that I never do as you tell me and am stubbornly resistant to even good advice,' Alexius fielded.

Rosie blinked in horror as flash bulbs went off all

around them, momentarily lighting them up and illuminating a sea of grinning faces.

'Alex…' she wailed, still in shock at his behaviour.

Alexius lowered her carefully into the rear of the waiting limousine and swung in beside her, watching with helpless amusement as she struggled to sit up and smooth back her tumbled hair from her flushed face. 'How could you do that to me?' she demanded wrathfully.

'You didn't give me a choice. The prospect of a couple of comic photographs doesn't bother me,' he admitted with a level of calm that disconcerted her.

'Where on earth are you taking me?' Rosie demanded sharply.

'Back to the island where we can fight in privacy.'

'I'm not going back to the island,' Rosie told him stonily.

'Please don't make me carry you through the airport kicking and screaming,' Alexius urged impatiently.

'I don't know what's come over you.'

'The knowledge that I don't have the right words to persuade you and that sometimes actions speak more loudly and truly,' he countered levelly.

'You didn't *try* to persuade me.'

'I told you I wanted you back.'

'*That* was persuasion?' Rosie was wide-eyed at the sheer primitive nature of that idea. 'I'll never forgive you for making a spectacle of us like this.'

Alexius contrived to look unconcerned by that warning and even dared to smile when Rosie got out of the limo at the airport and demonstrated no desire to run away. But then shock had overwhelmed Rosie's temper and made her think hard instead. She was very much

shaken by Alexius going to such extraordinary lengths
to try and get her back, even grudgingly impressed by
the level of importance he had to have attached to her
to act in such a way in public. And on one point he
was undeniably right: they did have to talk, had to sort
out their future relationship along civilised lines for
the baby's sake. Her grandfather's crack about 'sulking
teenagers' had hit a bull's eye with Rosie and made her
squirm with embarrassment.

Another barrage of cameras greeted them at the airport and she wondered bitterly if their colleagues outside the hotel had tipped them off. If they were hoping
for another show of some kind they were disappointed
when Alexius and Rosie merely walked decorously past.
They boarded the helicopter before Rosie remembered
her pet. 'Bas is at Grandad's!' she exclaimed in dismay.

'No, he's not. I took care of him before I arrived at
the party.'

Rosie shot his lean hard profile a frowning glance.
'What are you talking about?'

'Bas and your clothes were flown out earlier this
evening,' Alexius admitted reluctantly, watching the
gleam of incredulity spark in her eyes. 'I may not be
the romantic type but I am very practical, *glyka mou*.'

'And how did Bas greet you?'

'Like he would greet any kidnapper—with snarls and
snapping teeth! But I got him all the same,' Alexius informed her cheerfully. They were on their way back to
the island and he felt more energised than he had felt
all week. Although he still felt that he lacked the right
words and approach he was convinced that with persistence he could get over that barrier.

Momentarily weak, Rosie rested her pounding head

back against the seat rest. Why had he told Socrates to go ahead and announce their engagement? Did Alexius actually believe that he could railroad her into marriage? Was this her cue to accept that for their child's sake she had to settle for a guy who only wanted her to provide him with 'amazing' sex? Possibly she was guilty of expecting too much from Alexius. Nobody could love to order. Either love was there or it was not. He had had no business criticising her dress and behaviour at the party. What had come over him? She could have been forgiven for thinking that he was jealous.

Alexius…jealous? Her soft mouth formed a little moue of wry amusement, even as she conceded that she had been jealous of his apparent closeness to Yannina Demas. Seeing Alexius with another woman had been like having little knives shot deep into her shrinking flesh, she acknowledged painfully. But considering that he had walked out of the party leaving Yannina behind, she knew she had no grounds to be jealous.

Yet weeks had passed since she had faced the fact that if she did not marry Alexius there would be other women in his life. She couldn't have it both ways, she reminded herself doggedly. Either she married him or set him free, and if she married him she would have to accept that he would be something less than her dream husband. But then how many women got to marry their dream? Alexius was *her* dream even if she was not *his*. He didn't love her—her every regret came down to the same cruel bottom line and there was no escaping it. Could she live without his love? Would it be easier to accept a practical marriage than live without him? But then she wasn't living without him well… She was absolutely miserable without him.

It was the early hours of the morning when the helicopter landed on Banos. The big house was fully lit and Bas ran out of the front door barking an excited welcome. Rosie could barely move in her short skirt and Alexius simply laughed when he registered her predicament and lifted her out to set her down. Her high heels crunched across dew-wet grass up the steps and indoors. She scooped up Bas on the way, soothing his frantic licking and fussing with quiet words.

'You know, this has got to be the most insane thing you've ever done,' she told Alexius weakly in the echoing hall and then, in a tone that barely contained her incredulity and frustration, 'Why didn't you phone me?' she yelled at him.

'I didn't know what to say,' he muttered fiercely. 'I was scared I would make things worse and lose you for ever.'

And something gave within Rosie. *I was scared.* She had never thought he would admit to anything like that and it touched her deep and made her want to listen for a change.

'I can't stand this house without you in it,' he admitted abruptly as he strode into the drawing room. 'I had to *do* something.'

Lashes fluttering over her dazed eyes, Rosie followed him. 'The something was a bit extreme…'

'Not as far as I'm concerned,' Alexius asserted. 'My world comes alive when you're around but it's dead when you're not.'

Her eyes rounded. 'You missed me?'

'Of course I missed you! What do you think I am? A stone?'

'I have wondered sometimes.' Her fancy shoes pinching, Rosie sat down on an opulent sofa and kicked them off with a sigh of relief. He had missed her but he still hadn't been able to work himself up to a simple phone call. He was a mass of contradictions and complexities, some of which she might never grasp because she was a much more straightforward person.

He stood in front of formal marble fireplace, rigid with tension. 'I want you back. I want to marry you.'

'So you've said,' Rosie conceded, no longer sure what her answer should be, for over time the once clear lines of her rejection had blurred as she came to need him more and more.

Alexius released his breath in a slow hiss. 'We could have a good marriage. You and the baby would be the most important elements in my world.'

Rosie dealt him a frowning look of doubt. 'How can you say that?'

'It's the truth,' he declared, a slight flush highlighting his amazing cheekbones. 'The complete and utter truth, *moraki mou*.'

'And when did this…staggering change in your attitude come about?' Rosie prompted, desperate for him to convince her, absolutely pathetically desperate to make that leap.

'When you weren't here any more,' Alexius admitted jerkily. 'Somehow and right from the start you got under my skin—'

'Are you sure this isn't just a temporary condition?'

Alexius lifted his handsome head high, silver eyes screened, his discomfiture pronounced. 'I haven't looked at another woman since the day I met you.'

'You were with that Demas woman this evening,' Rosie reminded him, afraid to hope, afraid to believe.

'Nina called me to ask if she could go with me to the party. She's a friend, nothing more.'

'And you truly haven't slept with anyone else since you met me?' Rosie prompted shakily.

'Truly,' he affirmed gruffly. 'I don't want anyone else but you.'

Her heart hammered below her breastbone and soft pink lit her small face as she studied him, hope leaping high as the ceiling above. 'Then I could consider staying for good this time…'

Alexius nodded slowly, as restrained as she in his reaction. He dug into his pocket to produce a small jewellery box and crossed the room to offer it to her. 'It would make me very happy if you wore this.'

His formality took Rosie aback. *This* proved to be a magnificent diamond solitaire ring that glittered blindingly in the artificial light. She remembered him telling her grandfather to announce the engagement but she was still dumbfounded, not having expected Alexius to go for such a traditional approach. 'You're really serious about this, aren't you?' she whispered unsteadily, gently removing the ring from the box and sliding it onto the relevant finger. 'But you didn't need to get me a ring…'

'Yes, I did,' he disagreed. 'We've done everything else the wrong way round. I wanted to do this the right way.'

Rosie was enchanted by the way her ring caught the light. 'Who says it was the wrong way round?'

'I do. It took me too long to realise how much you meant to me… I nearly lost you,' Alexius told her grittily.

'I love you, Alex. I have from the start,' Rosie murmured with gentle dignity as she finally abandoned her defensive attitude. 'I'd be kind of hard to lose.'

He lifted her off the sofa in one swift movement to crush her against his big, powerful frame. 'I need you… I don't like my world without you in it. Is that love?'

'Only you can tell. I'm horribly unhappy when I have to wake up in the morning without you,' Rosie admitted ruefully. 'This past week—'

'—has been hell,' he cut in harshly, knotting one hand into the fall of her hair to tip her head back, staring down at her with diamond-bright eyes of tender appreciation and pleasure. 'I was counting the hours until I could see you again and then when I did see you, it all went wrong.'

'Yes,' she conceded. 'You had another woman with you.'

'And you didn't look like you any more in that fancy dress. I don't like other men looking at you. I'm very possessive when it comes to you and I've never felt that way before. It seemed so petty but I couldn't help it, and when you smiled at that creep you were dancing with I wanted to kill him!' he admitted grimly.

Rosie smiled up at him with wondering eyes, beginning to believe that he was hers at last, and more hers indeed than she had ever dreamt he might be. 'I love you, Alex.'

'We're going to get married as soon as it can be arranged,' Alexius told her squarely. 'Tell me now if you're going to fight about that.'

'I'm not going to fight. You need me, you care about me and I think you have room in your heart for the baby as well,' she said, happiness and hope twinned in her heart and blossoming.

'*Our* baby,' Alexius countered, sliding a hand below her skirt to splay his fingers across her stomach. 'You're getting bigger, *agape mou*. Knowing that's my baby in there is very sexy.'

Rosie trembled as his thumb stroked across her mound, awakening the awareness that his very presence teased with anticipation. He swept her up in his arms and headed for the stairs. 'You know, I don't know anything about being a father,' he warned her worriedly.

'And I don't know much more about being a mother,' she pointed out equably, stroking a calming hand along the hard angular curve of his jaw. 'We'll both learn as we go along. We have all the time in the world.'

He laid her down on his big wide bed with tremendous care. 'I know I love you and I'll never stop loving you. But it unnerves me to think that we might never have met.'

'But we *did* meet.' Rosie drew him down to her with determined hands, hungry for his kisses, eager to soothe his concerns and wrap him up tight in her love. 'And now we're together.'

'Together for ever,' Alexius rhymed, his tender gaze locked to her lovely face. 'I'm afraid you've got a life sentence, *agape mou*. You get no time off for good behaviour.'

'I can live with that but I can't live without you,' Rosie whispered on a soft sigh of pleasure as his sensual mouth covered hers.

EPILOGUE

Rosie descended the stairs of the villa on Banos. The big house had been modernised into a vision of stunning contemporary elegance soon after her marriage to Alexius. Her green designer dress was complimented by a breathtaking set of diamond jewellery reputed to have once belonged to the Russian royal family and a gift to her from her husband on their first anniversary. As she reached the hall, a little girl bowled up to her with Bas dancing at her heels.

'You look like a princess, Mummy,' Kasma opined. She was a very pretty little girl with a shock of black Stavroulakis curls and her mother's bright green eyes. Her enquiring mind, impish sense of humour and quick tongue were a mix of both parents. 'Great-grandad is in the drawing room. He looks very smart too.'

Socrates Seferis was enjoying a quiet drink by the fire. The party being hosted that night by his granddaughter and her husband was to mark the occasion of their fifth wedding anniversary. Time had been kind to the older man, for although his hair was now white, laughter lines were more prominent than frown lines in his weather-beaten face. His health had been good since his surgery, enabling him to continue at the helm of his hotel chain long enough to train Rosie into following in his footsteps.

Rosie and Alexius had settled in London after their wedding when she was five months pregnant with Kasma. Kasma had been born there and Rosie had not gone to university until her daughter was a year old. Basing themselves in the UK had made it easier for Rosie to study for her degree in business management. Alexius had had great plans for his wife to work alongside him after her graduation but a few weeks spent at her husband's elbow being told what to do every minute of the day had persuaded Rosie that they were not natural companions in an office environment. Instead, Rosie had gone to work for her grandfather and learn the hotel trade and together they had proved an unbeatable combination.

'You look wonderful,' her grandfather told her cheerfully. 'I made a wonderful match for you both, didn't I?'

Rosie's fine brows shot towards her hairline. 'What on earth do you mean?'

Socrates gave her a teasing little smile. 'When I saw that first photo of you after I had had you investigated, you reminded me so much of my late wife, your grandmother, that I prayed that you had inherited more than her looks. Alexius needed a down-to-earth woman who could make him a home and give him a family, not a fancy beauty more interested in shopping and socialising. That's why I urged him to look you up and get to know you for me…'

Rosie stared at him in shock, astounded that he could have been so manipulative. 'Are you serious?'

'Aren't you a marvellous fit for each other? Aren't you happy with him?' her grandfather prompted with unconcealed satisfaction. 'Well, then, it was worth the risk.'

Rosie smiled but she was really waiting for the sound of a single helicopter overhead, for Alexius was late. A fleet of helicopters would soon follow, ferrying most of their party guests out to the island for the celebration. Some of the guests were sailing in on their yachts.

'Aren't you having a drink?' Socrates asked.

'Not at the moment,' Rosie hedged, for she had news she wanted to share with Alexius first. Alexius, much to his surprise, had discovered that he really adored being a father and he was wonderful with Kasma, but the extreme busyness of their lives had made extending the family too much of a challenge until recently. Now that they were spending more time in Greece and on the island, the pace of their lives had slowed down. They had had more time to be together as a family, as a couple. Her eyes took on a dreamy hue as she recognised the thwack-thwack noise of the helicopter approaching.

'Go ahead,' Socrates advised with amusement as she shifted her feet restively. 'Don't mind me. He loves it when you rush outside to welcome him home!'

Rosie required no second bidding. She went to the front door, stepped out onto the brightly lit verandah, its undeniable charm carefully conserved during the renovation, and hurried down the steps. The big craft was just landing and she waited on the lawn for her first glimpse of Alexius. He sprang out of the helicopter: big, dark, devastatingly handsome, *hers*, and her heart leapt with the happiness as much a part of her now as her ready smile and laughter.

'You're late,' she told the light of her life nonetheless.

Alexius sent her a slashing grin of amusement. 'I had

to collect your present before I left Athens. You look shockingly beautiful, Mrs Stavroulakis.'

'I should—it was a shockingly expensive dress, and let's not forget the diamonds,' she urged ruefully.

'Will you never learn to accept a compliment gracefully?' he teased as he urged her up the steps into the house with Bas making sneak attacks on his trouser legs.

'Probably not.'

Pausing only to greet Socrates and Kasma, who had parked herself on her great-grandfather's lap with her favourite storybook, Alexius swept his wife upstairs to their room and kissed her breathless, pausing to look down at her with adoring eyes and a certain question.

'No, we don't have time,' she informed him firmly, subduing the surge of heat at her feminine core, ignoring the tightening of her tender breasts.

He stripped without ceremony and headed into the shower, talking all the way, telling her what he had been doing, whom he had met, what they had said with the new openness that had begun to dissolve his reserve soon after their marriage. He trusted her, he valued her, he *needed* her. Rosie was aware of her husband's love in a hundred different ways every day of their marriage.

'Happy anniversary, *agape mou*,' Alexius breathed when he was fully dressed. 'Your present's downstairs.'

'Yours is right here.' Rosie patted her stomach complacently.

Disconcerted, Alexius blinked and then his stunning silver eyes shone with brilliance as he grasped her meaning. 'We're pregnant?'

'We are,' Rosie confirmed proudly. 'I haven't told Grandad yet.'

'You wonderful, wonderful woman,' Alexius told her with his heart in his eyes.

They walked downstairs hand in hand to find Kasma and Bas hovering over a pet carrier in the hall.

'Your present,' Alexius explained, bending down to unlock the door of the carrier just as a shrill little bark sounded within.

A tiny white chihuahua puppy bounced out, barking like mad at Bas when he got too close in his efforts to investigate this strange spectacle.

'I thought it was time that Bas got the chance to enjoy the civilising effects of sharing his life with a good woman,' Alexius divulged with a wicked smile tugging at the corners of his charismatic mouth that only deepened as the aggressive advances of the lively puppy drove Bas into retreat below an occasional table.

Rosie laughed and wrapped her arms round her husband. 'Is that what I did to you? Drove you into retreat?'

'But I came out fighting,' Alexius breathed, closing his arms round her and kissing her in spite of their daughter's revolted kissy-kissy sounds behind them. 'I love you so much.'

'And I love you,' Rosie murmured, her heart still racing while she thought about the guests due to arrive and the party still to come, all those hours to be got through before she could be alone with the man she loved again. Anticipation, however, brought an edge to the excitement that he never failed to arouse.

* * * * *

#3117 IN THE HEAT OF THE SPOTLIGHT
The Bryants: Powerful & Proud
Kate Hewitt
Ambitious tycoon Luke Bryant's power and passion will lay scandalous Aurelie bare.... She's determined not to let him get beneath her skin, but faced with the sexiest man she's ever met, Aurelie can't resist just one touch!

#3118 NO MORE SWEET SURRENDER
Scandal in the Spotlight
Caitlin Crews
Ivan Korovin's only solution to a PR nightmare created by outspoken Miranda Sweet is to give the ravenous public what they want—to see these two enemies become lovers! But soon the mutually beneficial charade becomes too hot to handle!

#3119 PRIDE AFTER HER FALL
Lucy Ellis
Lorelai is an heiress on the edge, hiding her desperation behind her glossy blond hair and even brighter smile. Legendary racing driver Nash Blue never could resist a challenge—and he begins his biggest yet: unwrapping the real Lorelai St James....

#3120 LIVING THE CHARADE
Michelle Conder
When buttoned-up Miller Jacob needs to find a fake boyfriend, Valentino Ventura, maverick of the racing world, is the last person she wants. Up for the job, Valentino can't wait to help Miller let her hair—and whatever else she wants—down!

REQUEST YOUR FREE BOOKS!

HARLEQUIN *Presents*

PASSION GUARANTEED SEDUCTION

2 FREE NOVELS PLUS
2 FREE GIFTS!

YES! Please send me 2 FREE Harlequin Presents® novels and my 2 FREE gifts (gifts are worth about $10). After receiving them, if I don't wish to receive any more books, I can return the shipping statement marked "cancel." If I don't cancel, I will receive 6 brand-new novels every month and be billed just $4.30 per book in the U.S. or $4.99 per book in Canada. That's a saving of at least 14% off the cover price! It's quite a bargain! Shipping and handling is just 50¢ per book in the U.S. and 75¢ per book in Canada.* I understand that accepting the 2 free books and gifts places me under no obligation to buy anything. I can always return a shipment and cancel at any time. Even if I never buy another book, the two free books and gifts are mine to keep forever.

106/306 HDN FVRK

Name _____ (PLEASE PRINT)

Address _____ Apt. #

City _____ State/Prov. _____ Zip/Postal Code

Signature (if under 18, a parent or guardian must sign)

Mail to the **Harlequin® Reader Service:**
IN U.S.A.: P.O. Box 1867, Buffalo, NY 14240-1867
IN CANADA: P.O. Box 609, Fort Erie, Ontario L2A 5X3

**Are you a current subscriber to Harlequin Presents books
and want to receive the larger-print edition?
Call 1-800-873-8635 or visit www.ReaderService.com.**

* Terms and prices subject to change without notice. Prices do not include applicable taxes. Sales tax applicable in N.Y. Canadian residents will be charged applicable taxes. Offer not valid in Quebec. This offer is limited to one order per household. Not valid for current subscribers to Harlequin Presents books. All orders subject to credit approval. Credit or debit balances in a customer's account(s) may be offset by any other outstanding balance owed by or to the customer. Please allow 4 to 6 weeks for delivery. Offer available while quantities last.

Your Privacy—The Harlequin® Reader Service is committed to protecting your privacy. Our Privacy Policy is available online at www.ReaderService.com or upon request from the Harlequin Reader Service.

We make a portion of our mailing list available to reputable third parties that offer products we believe may interest you. If you prefer that we not exchange your name with third parties, or if you wish to clarify or modify your communication preferences, please visit us at www.ReaderService.com/consumerschoice or write to us at Harlequin Reader Service Preference Service, P.O. Box 9062, Buffalo, NY 14269. Include your complete name and address.

*When Selene asks her father's most hated business rival
for help, she has no idea what it will cost her!
Read on for a scintillating sneak-peek from USA TODAY
bestselling author Sarah Morgan's incredible new book,
SOLD TO THE ENEMY.*

* * *

STEFAN stared at her, his eyes sweeping her face for clues
and suddenly he stilled. Those beautiful washed-green
eyes were a rare color he'd seen only once before. "Selene?
Selene Antaxos."

"You *do* recognize me."

"Barely." His eyes swept her frame. "You've…grown."
He remembered her as an awkward teenager completely
dominated by her overprotective father. A pampered princess never allowed out of her heavily guarded palace.

Stay away from my daughter, Ziakas.

Just thinking of the name Antaxos was enough to ruin his
day, and now here was the daughter, standing in his office.

Dark emotion rippled through him, unwelcome and
unwanted.

He reminded himself that the daughter wasn't responsible for the sins of the father.

"Why are you dressed as a nun?"

"I had to sneak past my father's security."

"I can't imagine that was easy. Of course if your father
didn't make so many enemies, he wouldn't need an entire
army to protect him." Blocking the feelings that rose inside
him, he stood up and strolled round his desk. "What are you
doing here?"

She bent down and caught hold of the hem of her habit.

"Do you mind if I take this off? It's really hot and there's no point in keeping it on now I'm safe with you."

Knowing that most women considered him anything but "safe," Stefan watched in stunned disbelief as she wriggled and struggled until finally she freed herself, emerging with her hair in tangled disarray. Underneath she was wearing a white silk shirt teamed with a smart black pencil skirt that hugged legs designed to turn a man's mind to pulp.

"Does your father know you're here?"

"What do you think?" The corner of her mouth dimpled into a naughty smile, and Stefan stared, hypnotized by her lips, trying to clear his mind of wicked thoughts.

"I think your father must be having a few sleepless nights."

Come into my house, Little Red Riding Hood, and close the door behind you.

* * *

Can Selene deal with the devil and escape unscathed? Find out what happens when the door closes behind Selene on January 22, 2013, from Harlequin Presents®!

HARLEQUIN *Presents*®

*She's determined to uncover the secret
he's been keeping...*

New from *USA TODAY* bestselling author

Melanie Milburne

Edoardo Silveri can't believe the furious woman
standing before him is Bella Haverton—his ward!
But the pounding of her fist against the door is
rivaled only by the pounding coursing through his
body at the sight of this passionate beauty.
If Bella thinks she can break his hold, she's got
another thing coming. Doesn't she know that he
always rises to a challenge?

UNCOVERING
THE SILVERI SECRET

Available January 22, 2013.

www.Harlequin.com

HP13120